Title Page

August 23, 1864:
The Day Abraham Lincoln Won the Civil War

Rev. 02/15/2026

Feedback: alsnewideas@gmail.com

Other books by Alan Sewell

https://www.amazon.com/Alan-Sewell/e/B00557PQDY

Contents

Foreword

This is the story of the most decisive day of the Civil War. Although novelized, it is substantially true and documented in the historical record. I first researched the story for articles I wrote for *Civil War Times Illustrated Magazine* for its December 1981 special edition *Dissent: Fire in the Rear.*

The story was said to be provocative then, and seems to remain so today, after nearly 40 years of additional research and writing. Perhaps because it introduces complexities into the study of Civil War history that have seldom been explored. I believe these aspects are important because they give life to Mr. Lincoln's wisdom and fortitude in transforming what could have been a crippling day for the Union into the day that restored the Union Government's course to victory.

This day was the lowest point of the Union's fortunes. Grant's army was losing as many as 15,000 men *per week* killed, wounded, captured, or died of disease, or were discharged for illness. It would be equivalent to the modern United States suffering 225,000 military casualties *per week*. The Confederates had lost territory and men, but they were not defeated. In fact, they felt they were gaining the upper hand. Morale in Robert E. Lee's army was high.

Morale in the North faltered. Pro-Confederate "Copperheads" were elected to majorities in several Northern state legislatures, including Mr. Lincoln's home state of Illinois. Forcible conscription of unwilling draftees up to age 45 stirred resentment and defiance. Lincoln called it "The Fire in the Rear, more dangerous than the open Rebellion in the South." He'd been elected in 1860 with only 39% of the popular vote. He seemed even less popular now that the war was deep into its fourth, and bloodiest, year. He expected to lose the upcoming election to George McClellan, a pre-war protégé of Jefferson Davis. He expected McClellan, if elected, would sign an armistice with the Confederates implicitly recognizing their independence.

At the beginning of this day he wrote a memo despairing of re-election. He decided to send a commissioner to Richmond to discuss peace with Jefferson Davis. However, as the day wore on, he was called upon to make decisions that would ultimately decide the course of the election and the war. In retrospect, this day was seen to be the turning point of the war.

He completed the memorandum he'd written to himself. Various reports had it that he would fail of re-election. His former subordinate, General George B. McClellan, dismissed from command of the Union armies two years ago, was running against him. The Democrats' platform called for an end to hostilities, hoping the Confederates would reenter the Union voluntarily. A forlorn hope, he believed, but many families in the North, grieving the deaths of sons, fathers, brothers, and husbands, were desperate for peace. He read the memorandum he'd written to himself a final time, then signed it:

Executive Mansion,
Washington, Aug. 23, 1864.

This morning, as for some days past, it seems exceedingly probably that this Administration will not be re-elected. Then it will be my duty to so co-operate with the President. President. elect, so to save the Union between the election and the inauguration; as he will have secured his election on such ground that he cannot possibly save it afterwards.

A. Lincoln.

This morning, as for some days past, it seems exceedingly probable that this administration will not be re-elected. Then it will be my duty to so cooperate with the new President-elect as to save the Union between the election and the inauguration, as he will have secured his election on such ground that he cannot possibly save it afterwards.

He folded it in thirds, placed it in an envelope adorned with Union flags, and closed the flap. He placed a spoon of sealing wax over the lamp on his desk, then poured the melted wax over the back of the envelope, embossing it with the presidential seal. He looked at the envelope, sighed, penned the date, and put it in the bottom drawer of his desk. He vowed not to open it until the day after the election in eleven weeks.

Half-filled coffee mugs shoved into a corner cabinet bore testimony to the long hours he'd spent here. On the mantle between their desks was an ice cabinet whose cool air wafted down on the floor, then rose on the draft from the transom. On the other side of the room, the window fogged with the humidity of the oppressive Washington summer. It was only a quarter-till-nine, but already the sun was high enough to set the ground steaming. He leaned back, closed his eyes, and thought through the issues he'd have to confront on this most difficult day of his life.

If he decided them incorrectly, future historians would measure him by his mistakes. They would argue about whether he'd been too slow to remove McClellan from command of the armies, or too quick; whether he'd been too tardy in emancipating the Rebels' slaves, or too precipitant; whether he'd been tyrannical in waging a harsh war or whether he'd been too fastidious in obeying every letter of the Constitution. Of course, he didn't have to wait for the judgements of historians. He was judged harshly enough in the present.

The patriotism animating the North during the days following Fort Sumter was drowned in the torrents of blood and disease that killed and crippled hundreds, sometimes thousands, of Union soldiers each day. Democrats heavily defeated Lincoln's Republicans in the elections of 1862, electing peace-minded "Copperheads" to Congress and the state legislatures of the Northern states from New York to Lincoln's own shaky Illinois, where only five of the fourteen congressional seats remained Republican.

He'd won his home state in 1860 with 50.8% of the vote and lost his hometown of Springfield. The Democrats had been divided into three competing factions and spent as much time campaigning against each other as they had against him, enabling to squeak by with just under 40% of the popular vote. They were united now, under the fiction of ending the war they said he started and restoring the Union through

9

compromise he would not make. An outrageous fiction, he presumed, but people under duress might convince themselves to believe it. Would he have to face the ultimate humiliation of losing the war, the election including his home state, and suffer until the last day of his life, the agony of losing a third of the country, with himself being blamed as the agent of its catastrophe?

Northern Copperheads:
In favor of a vigorous prosecution of peace!

These Copperheads wore buttons making clear their view that the South was winning the war, and peace must be made on the Confederates' terms:

Secretary of War Stanton had shown him the vile literature the pro-Confederate Northern Copperhead press was distributing:

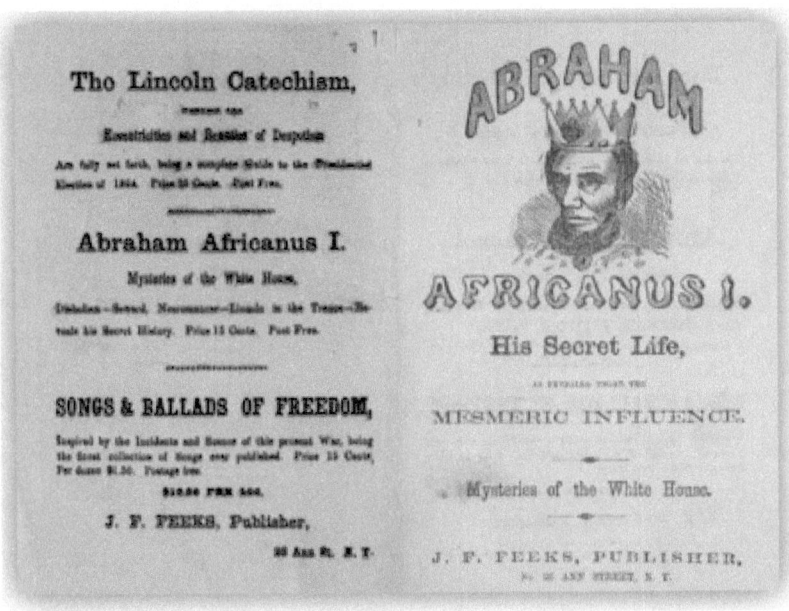

They made their nest in the Democrats' Party, becoming emboldened to hold their convention in Chicago, the city where

Republicans had nominated Mr. Lincoln in 1860. Their presumed nominee was former General George McClellan, the protégé of Jefferson Davis when Davis was Secretary of War during Franklin Pierce's administration. Lincoln expected that if the two ever got together to talk peace, it would be concluded on Jefferson Davis's terms of Confederate independence.

With desertions running around seven thousand per month, and recruitment failing to replace the losses from fifteen thousand battle casualties during each week of heavy fighting, Mr. Lincoln feared McClellan's election would provoke the dissolution of the Union armies. What could he do to make his failure of re-election less "exceedingly probable?"

John Hay, Lincoln's young secretary from his law-office days back in Springfield, came bounding into his office on schedule. Hay's desk, also overflowing with correspondence, had a copy book and press to duplicate Mr. Lincoln's letters before they left the White House. An early riser, he had filled the ice cabinet before Mr. Lincoln arrived, then gone downstairs to interview the people in the White House waiting room who hoped to see the president.

"How's the Tycoon today?"

Lincoln opened his eyes. "Fine enough to keep house, I reckon."

"You don't look so fine," observed Hay. "If the rings under your eyes were any bigger, I'd think a raccoon had usurped your office!"

Mr. Lincoln smiled broadly. Some of Mr. Hay's boundless optimism always seemed to rub off on him.

"I feel better than I may look, young fellow. How many people are waiting downstairs?"

"About thirty, more or less."

"Who has the most urgent business?"

"Those five sergeants the Rebels paroled out of Andersonville are hankerin' to see you. They implore you to resume the prisoner exchanges. They say there's eighty to a hundred of our boys dying in that hellhole every day."

Lincoln shook his head. He'd already declined their request to see him when they'd entered the Federal lines the day before yesterday. They came to Washington anyway, hoping he'd change his mind. The Confederates had given them passes to come up from wretched Andersonville to plead for a resumption of the prisoner exchanges, disrupted last year when the Confederates refused to exchange black Union soldiers they'd captured, returning those who'd escaped slavery to their former owners. The Confederates had relented on exchanging black Union prisoners since then, but now General Grant didn't want the prisoner exchange resumed.

"I can't see them, John. If I did, I'm afraid my heart would weaken so much, that I'd have to agree to resume the prisoner exchange. Grant says exchanging prisoners helps the Rebs more than us. Their men are enlisted for the duration of the war. Ours are enlisted for terms of one to three years, and some for only a hundred days. Most go home after they're exchanged. Resuming the prisoner exchange would put another Rebel army in the field without doing much to augment ours. Grant says if we don't win this war by next summer, we'll have to concede the Rebels' independence. We can't let them prolong the war by getting their men back."

"Those sergeants have the look of death in their eyes," implored Hay. "Can't you at least see them? They came all this way from living hell, and they're only a staircase away. Can't you tell them to wait here a few weeks while you consider it, so they can get some meat on their bones before they have to go back to that hellhole?"

Lincoln shook his head again. "I'd just be deceiving them, while having the sorrow of that decision weighing down on me. Of course, it's up to them if they want to break their parole and stay here."

"They're men of honor," responded Hay. "They say they're going back to Andersonville tomorrow if you won't see them. Said they'd rather die there, starving and wallowing in filth, than go back on their word. Pity they'll have to go all the way back there knowing that every step takes them closer to the grave."

"Men of honor," repeated Lincoln. The creases on his head deepened. "We must suppress this Rebellion, so we'll never again have to waste the lives of men of honor!

"Who else has an urgent case to see me about?"

15

"A woman says her husband is going to be shot for desertion. Says he'll be shot at sundown Friday unless you pardon him. Most of the others want to ask you for appointments to customs and post offices. A few are requesting passes to see their families in the South. A couple from the South are here to ask you to order the return their properties we've confiscated for delinquent taxes."

"I'll see the woman. Tell the rest I can't see them today. I've got a cabinet meeting at eleven, an address to an Ohio company at one-thirty, a heap of correspondence to catch up on, and guests this afternoon and evening. Please tell the Andersonville men that I've heard their request, but I can't act on it. Don't tell them anything else. I'm not at liberty to discuss the motives behind my decision."

Mr. Hay returned with the woman whose husband was to be executed.

"Mr. President, Mrs. Mina Bohm, from Herkimer County, New York."

A shabbily dressed middle-aged woman entered and nodded her head.

"How do you do sir? My husband Dolf is scheduled to be killed Friday. He's forty-five years old. We're poor country folks. He didn't have no money to buy his way out of the draft like the well-to-do men in town. Please, sir, spare his life. He don't feel spritely, like when he was young. He never should've been in the army."

"I understand he deserted," said Lincoln. "I've never known my officers to execute men for their first desertion. What else did he do?"

The woman cried. "He's tried to come home twicen' before, sir. Like I said, he don't belong in the army."

"Where is he being held?"

"He's in Grant's Army. I don't know nothing more than that. He asked someone to write me a letter. The postmaster knowed it was somethin' serious. He brought it out to our farm and read it to me. Otherwise, I wouldn't have knowed about it 'till after Dolf was dead. He's to be killed at sunset Friday evening. I came here straight away, prayin' all the way that I'd get here in time to see you before the deed was done. Please, sir, Dolf's a Union man. But he don't belong being in the army. Not at his age."

He must be a spry old goat if he's run off from the army three times.

But her words, "He's to be killed" had shaken him. He looked into Mrs. Bohm's eyes, seeing her fear of losing her husband to the disgraceful death of military execution, and spending the rest of her miserable life as a lonely widow in the poorhouse.

What am I to do? Congress has passed the Enrollment Act, requiring men up to 45 to enlist or pay the commutation fee of $300. I doubt the Bohms have ever seen $300 in their lives. We have forced him into the army when wealthier men have paid to avoid the obligation. But that is the law. If I pardon him, then I have negated the Act of Congress, and have been unfair with other men his age who have been compelled to service and have not deserted. No doubt some have been killed or severely wounded in battle or have died of disease. If I pardon this man, then what can I say to the widows of the dutiful men his age who are killed or crippled while faithfully carrying out their duty?

He closed his eyes and sighed.

But if word gets around that we're killing old men in cold blood, and leaving their widows without support, we'll lose the election and the war.

"Do you have the letter?" he asked Mrs. Bohm.

"Oh, yes, sir! Here it is," she said, pulling the letter from her bag.

He squinted at the letter, in barely legible handwriting, stained with mud and rain. He discerned "Adolf Bohm, 121st New York Rgt. sentenced to be shot for desertion on sunset August 26th, 1864."

He took his pen out of the ink well and wrote on White House stationary:

Executive Mansion,
Washington, D.C.

August 23, 1864

To General U. S. Grant,

I am appealed to by Mina Bohm on behalf of her husband Adolf Bohm, of the 121st New York, who is under sentence to be shot as a deserter this Friday. He is represented to me to be forty-five years old and in poor health. If he has no other charges outstanding, I ask that you commute his sentence to parole to his home, for the duration of the War. Please confirm your receipt of this message, and the release of Mr. Bohm, promptly.

A. Lincoln.

To General U.S. Grant. Aug 23, 1864

I am appealed to by Mina Bohm on behalf of her husband Adolf Bohm, of the 121st New York, who is under sentence to be shot as a deserter this Friday. He is represented to me to be forty-five years old and in poor health. If he has no other charges outstanding, I ask that you commute his sentence to parole to his home, for the duration of the War. Please confirm your receipt of this message, and the release of Mr. Bohm, promptly.

"Take this, along with the letter, to Secretary Stanton's office," he told Mrs. Bohm. "Ask him to telegraph it to Grant's headquarters without delay. Wait there for confirmation that the order has been acknowledged and that your husband is released. If there are no other charges pending against, him, he will be paroled to your home for the duration of the war."

The woman cried. "Oh, thank you, sir, thank you so much."

"Please escort Mrs. Bohm to the War Department," he told Hay. "And see that her message is transmitted. Tell Secretary Stanton that she is to remain in his offices until he receives confirmation that Mr. Bohm has been released."

He rose to stretch his legs by walking to the other side of his office and peering out the window toward the Treasury Building. The ice bucket, bless it, had cooled the room enough to cause the window to fog from the oppressive heat outside. Thankfully, he couldn't smell the vile air outside rising from livestock and shallow cesspools. He strolled down the hall to the living quarters where ten-year old Tad was being tutored. His teacher was listening to him recite words from his spelling book.

When Tad saw his father, he put down his book and picked up a pistol captured from the Confederates. With the other hand he grabbed a Union Flag his father had given him. "Surrender, General Lee!" he shouted.

Mr. Lincoln laughed. "If only my generals had your spirit, this war would soon be won!"

He went downstairs to greet Mrs. Lincoln, supervising the preparations for dinner. Frederick Douglass, the Negro Abolitionist, was due at 4:30. She didn't know if he would be staying for dinner. General Lew Wallace, the hero of the Battle of Monocacy that saved Washington from Rebel capture in July, would be arriving for dinner at six. Mary grabbed a coffee pot off the stove and poured her husband's coffee, which she'd done every morning they'd been together in their twenty-one years of marriage.

"Thank you, Mother!" He inhaled the steamy aroma and cautiously sipped the hot brew. "This is excellent coffee. We're doing better than the Confederates on that score. I hear they're making their coffee out of bark and acorns."

"Proves I was right to go to Illinois and marry you instead of going off with my sisters to Alabama and ending up married to one of those Rebel scoundrels, doesn't it?"

"Well, you did run the risk of marrying Stephen Douglas in Illinois. He was a-courtin' you pretty vigorously. Good thing I came along when I did. You'd be a widow woman now if you'd married him."

Mrs. Lincoln wrinkled her nose. "I never could have married him, not after I saw him spit tobacco on that dance floor. You have your rough edges, but at least I educated you on how to act in civilized company."

He smiled. "You didn't think it possible to teach an old Illinois Sucker the manners of High Society, did you now?"

Mary sniffed. "I've trained horses, so I figured I could learn you passable manners." She gave a mock jerk of her head.

He hugged his wife. He did not do it often. She was often disturbed by bad temper bordering on insanity. The White House staff called her "The Hellcat." It was a rare moment when she adorned the mantle of their marriage with happiness.

Last year Mr. Lincoln had heard an appeal for clemency for another man sentenced to death for desertion. "Does he have a wife?" Lincoln asked. When the answer was affirmative, he'd replied: "Then I'll send him home to her. In a year, he'll wish I'd had him executed."

Besides her temper, Mary was extravagant. Yesterday, Secretary of War Stanton had informed him that she'd asked for a disbursement from the War Department to pay for dresses she'd bought in New York and Philadelphia. The bill was over $2,000, as much as Mr. Lincoln had earned in months of law practice before becoming president. Stanton said he'd told her that he could not reimburse her with War Department money because the government would lose the confidence of the people if it became corrupted by reimbursing private expenditures with public money.

He wondered if he should confront her about the conversation. She was emotionally unstable, swinging from euphoria to despair. She still grieved over the death of their beloved son Willie from typhoid fever a year and a half ago. She was distressed by Washington's high society disdain for her, though she was responsible for some of it, after she'd made enemies wielding her sharp tongue against the wives of Congressmen and Senators. The newspapers ridiculed her extravagance, while Washington society women spread malicious gossip about her. Some said she was a Confederate spy. He'd had to go before a secret congressional committee to testify under oath that she was loyal.

He sympathized with her, even though he was the most common victim of her tantrums.

Why can't they leave her alone? We are waging war for our nation's existence, and the gossipmongers have nothing better to do than savage Mary? I have often praised the wisdom of the people that allows them to choose our government. I hope I have not been overstating the case. People can act as foolish as cattle, and considerably meaner.

In her own way, Mary helped him and the Union cause. Against all odds, she'd befriended irascible old bachelor Senator Charles Sumner, the most radical Abolitionist in the Senate. He adored Mary's company, and she likewise admired his stern intellect. Maybe they got along so well because of their mutually offensive temperaments. He wondered if Sumner's affection for Mary might have prevented the Radical Republicans, who feared he was destined to lose the election, from nominating Salmon Chase to replace him. He could hardly blame them since he'd just written a memo to himself forecasting that result. For some reason, they hadn't gotten around to removing him yet. Maybe Sumner had something to do with that.

The better side of Mary's fickle nature shone brightly at the soldiers' hospitals where she enjoyed playing the motherly role to sick and wounded soldiers. Gravely wounded men smiled and laughed and cheered her when she visited, reminding them that their womenfolk were waiting to greet them as heroes when they won the war to save the nation. She also raised money for indigent Negroes who'd escaped slavery. Born into a Kentucky slave-owning family, she put to shame the hypocrisy of some Northerners who talked all the time about Negro equality but never let a colored person enter their home except as a servant. Had her unwavering loyalty to Mr. Lincoln and his cause persuaded the slaveowners in Missouri, Maryland, Delaware, and Kentucky to remain in the Union instead of following the rest of the Southern Slave States into the Confederacy?

He decided to confront her gently. He motioned her to follow him into the pantry room and closed the door. By the worried look on her face she could tell that Stanton had told him about the dresses.

"Mr. Stanton told me he talked with you about your expenses yesterday."

"Oh, Father, he shouldn't have told you about that!"

"Don't worry, Mother. I know you want to look your best when we are entertaining Washington society, and when we are meeting the public. That's important. The people want to see you in your most beautiful form."

Mrs. Lincoln beamed. "You know I am doing it for you."

"I know, and I am proud of you."

"But how will you pay my bills? Being president doesn't make us wealthy."

He patted her shoulder. "I'll work something out." *I'll take out a personal loan from Stanton or Gideon Welles.* "Why don't you see how Tad's doing with his reading and spelling? And thank you for the coffee."

Mrs. Lincoln looked as if she'd received a reprieve as joyous as Mr. Bohm's.

10:00 AM: Correspondence

He returned to his office. Hay was waiting there with the daily correspondence, the same as he'd delivered each morning since he and Mr. Lincoln arrived in the White House three and half years ago.

"What glad tidings have you brought me today?" he asked Hay with the accustomed half-smiling face of mixed sarcasm and humor.

Hay set down the correspondence on Lincoln's desk. The regular mail delivered by the post office arrived in sealed envelopes if confidential or as folded paper with a stamp glued on if it wasn't. Mailing envelopes were a recent invention. Few people used them unless they were conveying privileged information.

Three envelopes, containing the most important letters, were delivered by couriers.

The War Department telegrams came bundled in a string-tied package. Some were transmitted in cypher from the battle fronts, then deciphered by War Department officers and transcribed in their handwriting. He cut the strings with a letter opener, broke the wax seal, and let the telegrams spill on his desk. He gathered them up and patted them together, bent them, and let them roll off his thumb like a deck of cards.

He rubbed his head, damp with sweat despite the ice-cooled air pooling around him, then picked them up. On top of the stack was a dispatch from Grant reporting mixed results in Virginia. Grant said his men had occupied a part of the Weldon Railroad in hard fighting yesterday, that would force the Confederates to unload their trains short of Petersburg and haul them into Lee's lines by wagon, attenuating an already strained supply line on the Rebel front between there and Richmond.

However, Grant reported the loss of 4,300 men, including 3,000 missing and presumed captured. That was worrisome. The Army of the Potomac wasn't what it had been the year before at Gettysburg. Those men who had turned back Robert E. Lee on Cemetery Ridge were mostly gone from the army. Mr. Lincoln cyphered that in all the armies, about 250,000 experienced soldiers who'd fought at Gettysburg and the Western battles had been removed from the Union ranks during the last year, counting deaths from combat and disease, discharges with wounds and disease, captured, deserted, and those who enlisted in 1861 for three years and mustered out.

He made a quick calculation, as he was prone to doing after reading battle reports Grant's army lost four percent of its effective strength yesterday. If that kept up, the army would be extinguished in twenty-five days.

I used to say that sending men to General McClellan was like shoveling fleas across a barnyard. Few ever saw a battle. Grant is using all I send him, but getting them killed, wounded, and captured in numbers the public would not have stood for two years ago, and will not stand for much longer now.

Many still in the battle line weren't healthy enough to undertake long marches or assaults on Rebel fieldworks. Although the North was wealthy in industry and agriculture, it was difficult to keep the soldiers clothed, fed, and sheltered in the stinking Virginia mud and blistering sun, where battles raged almost every day, and sharpshooters picked off men bringing up supplies. Malnutrition, filth, and combat stress weakened the men physically and mentally.

The army's leadership was also in decline. Some of the best generals who'd won at Gettysburg, including corps commanders John Reynolds, John Buford, and John Sedgwick, were dead. Winfield Hancock, who'd steadied the Union lines atop Cemetery Ridge with his cool courage under fire, was severely wounded and no longer the confident leader he'd been. Deaths, wounds, and captures of experienced officers at the division, brigade, regimental levels, and company levels rendered the army sluggish and reluctant to attack.

As a result of this debilitation, Grant's army was losing battles it would have won last year. Some, like The Crater and Cold Harbor, were staggering defeats caused by bungling incompetence. Others petered out because the men lacked strength to move forward. The more Grant fought, the more the deficiencies compounded. The 4,300 experienced men lost yesterday would be replaced, if at all, by conscripts and bounty-jumpers, a fair proportion of whom were ne'er-do-wells who would desert or surrender at the first opportunity.

This explains why Grant ordered Mr. Bohm executed, which goes against all prior precedent. He decided he had to make an example to discourage desertions. Still, I believe he should not have picked this broken-down old man to make an example of. However, I will not be as eager to pardon the next case. If deserters are not punished by the standards of military discipline, why should the brave men who stay in the lines put their lives at risk?

It also explains why Grant insists that the prisoner exchanges must not resume. The exchanges benefit the Rebels because their men are enlisted for the duration of the war, but there is more to it than that. Our men who were conscripted into the army, or enlisted only for the bounty money, are surrendering at the first opportunity, even knowing of the horrors of Rebel prison camps. If they thought they'd be quickly exchanged, half the army might surrender.

The next military telegram reported that Union-occupied Memphis had fallen to a raid by Confederate General Forrest. Forrest had captured five hundred Union soldiers and narrowly missed capturing two generals at their headquarters.

These raids dejected the North and cheered the South. They made it clear that while the Union could capture strongpoints in the Confederacy, it could not control the land or the people in between. In fact, the Union Government seemed to be losing control of territory in Missouri and Kentucky thought to have been secured. The Confederates were even stepping up their incursions into the North. On July 30th, they had occupied and burned Chambersburg, PA --- 25 miles from the Gettysburg battlefield of the previous year --- --- in retaliation for Union depredations in Virginia

The "granddaddy" of all Rebel raids came in the 2nd week of July when Jubal Early's Corps of Robert E. Lee's Army entered the District of Columbia within sight of the Capitol dome. He'd ridden out to Fort Stevens on the edge of town to watch the Rebels. One of their sharpshooters, too far away to know who he was shooting at, hit an army doctor in uniform standing right next to him. A Union officer who either hadn't recognized the president, or didn't care, shouted, "Get down you damn fool," maybe saving his life when the next bullet came whizzing in.

Luckily, some of the Hundred Days men commanded by General Lew Wallace had sacrificed themselves outside the city the day before. Most had been killed, wounded, or captured, but fought well under Wallace's command, holding the Rebels up for a day. They gained enough time for Grant to send two corps of his veterans back from Richmond, arriving barely in time to discourage the Rebels from fighting their way into the city. Nevertheless, the raid had shaken confidence in Lincoln's administration, while disrupting Grant's offensive against the Confederate capital.

The other telegrams were field reports not requiring responses. He was concerned there was nothing from Sherman down in Georgia. He did not know Sherman and fretted about his ability to command an army marching so deeply into the enemy's country. Reports from early in the war described Sherman as "excitable." He'd been relieved of command and sent home for telling newspaper reporters the cost of winning the war would be far greater than the public anticipated. The newspapers called him "insane" then, but now his early forecast of the war's brutal severity was proven spot-on.

Should he send Sherman a dispatch requesting a full report on his operations? He decided not to. Perhaps Sherman would take it as an interference in his command and react badly. Grant said he could be trusted to handle a large army moving into the heart of the Rebellion, so he decided to leave it at that.

He turned to the stack of letters delivered by regular mail. They were mostly requests by merchants wanting permission to go South and purchase property, especially cotton, the Union Government confiscated from Rebels; requests for appointments to customs posts and post offices; and a couple of letters of banal advice from people he did not know. He set those aside for Hay and his other secretaries Nicolay and Stoddard to deliver to the proper departments, answer themselves, or discard.

That left the envelopes delivered by couriers.

The first was an envelope encased in an outer box from his friend, Republican "War Governor" Richard Yates of Illinois. He was apprehensive about reading anything from Yates. Though the governor anchored Unionists in Illinois, he was prone to overreacting to provocations from anti-war Democrats. He had suspended Illinois' State Legislature, claiming it was full of Copperheads seeking to join Illinois to the Confederacy. Now he was requesting Lincoln to send "four regiments of veteran soldiers" to Springfield to protect his one-man government. He also wanted *The Chicago Times*, that he called a "Copperhead rag," suppressed by Union soldiers.

Although he viewed Yates as an alarmist, there was no denying some merit in his alarm:

34

It was true that the Illinois and Indiana legislatures had demanded a peace conference with the Confederacy before Yates and Morton disbanded them.

It was true that Lincoln's home state was shaky. He'd narrowly won it in 1860 over Stephen Douglas, who'd carried their joint hometown of Springfield along with most counties in central and southern Illinois.

It was true that people in Illinois as far north as Alton had talked about joining the Confederacy during those volatile days at the beginning of the war.

It was true that back in the 1830's pro-slavery men in Alton had murdered abolitionist Elijah Lovejoy after burning down his newspaper office, and that many in Illinois railed against Abolitionists today.

It was true that the Illinois Legislature had passed anti-vagrancy laws designed to arrest idle Negroes and hire them out as indentured servants.

It was true that there always seemed to be somebody in Alton or Edwardsville or Springfield or Joliet who'd get drunk and run around cheering for Jeff Davis. Some were Southern men who'd come up from Kentucky and Virginia before the war. Some were Northern-born men who despised him.

It was true, even now, that the Union army sometimes had to garrison railroad bridges in Southern Illinois and Indiana as if they were Rebel States. Thousands of deserters from the Union armies were said to be hiding out in the wild country of Southern Illinois and along the bluffs of the Mississippi. Conscription agents attempting to dragoon unwilling men into military service had been shot.

35

It was true that he had inflamed these people during the early years of the war by permitting his subordinates to impose martial law in the North, arresting Democratic political opponents and suppressing their newspapers. He'd since come to realize that these two-legged Copperheads, like their venomous namesake reptiles, were best rendered harmless by ignoring them. Why go into their nest to stir them up? Alas, Yates and Morton, and some Federal military officers, kept the Democrats riled up by arresting their candidates on dubious charges and provoking them with cannons pointed at their political rallies.

Were these Copperheads capable of organizing sufficiently to require him to recall soldiers from the South to suppress an insurrection in the North? He didn't think so, but Yates bolstered his case by including affidavits from mutual friends. The first was from Governor Oliver P. Morton in Indiana, who'd also suspended his state's Democrat-majority State Legislature:

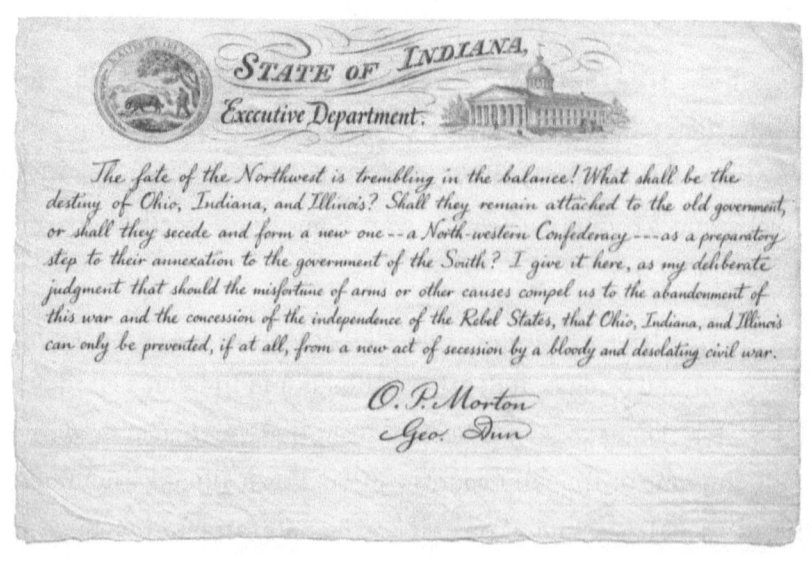

STATE OF INDIANA,

Executive Department.

The fate of the Northwest is trembling in the balance! What shall be the destiny of Ohio, Indiana, and Illinois? Shall they remain attached to the old government, or shall they secede and form a new one--a North-western Confederacy----as a preparatory step to their annexation to the government of the South? I give it here, as my deliberate judgment that should the misfortune of arms or other causes compel us to the abandonment of this war and the concession of the independence of the Rebel States, that Ohio, Indiana, and Illinois can only be prevented, if at all, from a new act of secession by a bloody and desolating civil war.

O. P. Morton
Geo. Dunn

The fate of the Northwest is trembling in the balance! What shall be the destiny of Ohio, Indiana, and Illinois? Shall they remain attached to the old government, or shall they secede and form a new one---a Northwestern Confederacy --- as a preparatory step to their annexation to the government of the South? I give it here, as my deliberate judgment that should the misfortune of arms or other causes compel us to the abandonment of this war and the concession of the independence of the Rebel States, that Ohio, Indiana, and Illinois can only be prevented, if at all, from a new act of secession by a bloody and desolating civil war.

Yates, always thorough, had a letter from another mutual friend, Illinois Congressman Elihu Washburne.

To the President,

Treason is everywhere bold, defiant, and active with impunity. In case of disaster, the Administration will be face to face with it, here in the North, and failing to meet it and overcome it, we are lost. Do not fancy this to be my own feelings, for I assure you we all here participate in them.

If we cannot speedily secure victories by our armies, peace must be made to secure us anything!

E. Washburne

Next came a letter from Joseph Medill, editor of Chicago's Republican newspaper, the *Chicago Tribune*:

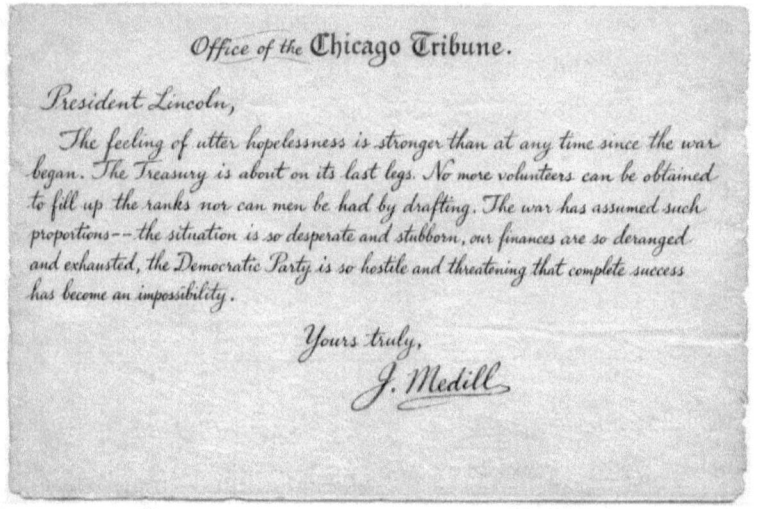

The feeling of utter hopelessness is stronger than at any time since the war began. The Treasury is about on its last legs. No more volunteers can be obtained to fill up the ranks nor can men be had by drafting. The war has assumed such proportions--- the situation is so desperate and stubborn, our finances are so deranged and exhausted, the Democratic Party is so hostile and threatening that complete success has become an impossibility.

The concurrence of opinion disturbed him but not to the point of acceding to Yates' request to bring back soldiers from the battle fronts to garrison Springfield. Nothing would demoralize Union men more than calling upon soldiers to defend their president's hometown from

Confederates! The opposition press was sure to lampoon a quivering Mr. Lincoln being escorted into his house by soldiers.

Instead, he decided to see what he could do about unobtrusively routing some Hundred Days Men through Springfield on their way back home. If it looked like trouble was brewing, they could detrain and settle it quickly and quietly.

As for suppressing the *Chicago Times*, he scanned the pages Yates enclosed, looking for overt evidence of treason. In May, the ever-vigilant Yates had alerted him by telegram to two anti-Lincoln papers in New York that conspired to publish and telegraph to other anti-Lincoln papers, a forged proclamation allegedly issued by Mr. Lincoln. The forged proclamation alleged Mr. Lincoln was demanding another 400,000 Northern men to be conscripted by force. It was purposed to incite more draft riots like the one in New York in July 1863, suppressed by artillery fire from New York artillery batteries called home after beating the Confederates out of Gettysburg. Mr. Lincoln recalled the lithographs of the hundreds killed right smack in the middle of the nation's preeminent city:

He'd therefore given stern orders for the suppression of the New York papers whose publishers and editors committed forgery against his administration:

Whereas there has been wickedly and traitorously printed and published this morning in the New York World and New York Journal of Commerce, newspapers printed and published in the city of New York, a false and spurious proclamation purporting to be signed by the President and to be countersigned by the Secretary of State, which publication is of a treasonable nature, designed to give aid and comfort to the enemies of the United States and to the rebels now at war against the Government and their aiders and abettors, you are therefore hereby commanded forthwith to arrest and imprison in any fort or military prison in your command, the editors, proprietors, and publishers of the aforesaid newspapers, and all such persons as, after public notice has been given of the falsehood of said publication, print and publish the same with intent to give aid and comfort to the enemy; and you will hold the persons so arrested in close custody until they can be brought to trial before a military commission for their offense.

However, he did not discern overt forgeries tending toward treason in these pages from *The Chicago Times,* only a tenor of harping criticism --- some perhaps even true --- of Yates running an unconstitutional state government on his sole authority after the suspension of the state legislature. Of Mr. Lincoln's governance, the paper alleged military incompetence in prosecuting the war and political malfeasance in failing to negotiate a peaceful return of the Confederacy to the Union, alleging that "War for the Union has ended, and War for the Negro begun." That sort of talk had been enough for Mr. Lincoln to allow his military governors to suppress the paper in 1862.

"Must I shoot a simple soldier for deserting his post," he asked, "while not harming a hair the wily agitator who encouraged him to desert?"

He'd therefore been aggressive in ordering the military to arrest outspoken opponents, including pro-Confederate members of the Maryland state legislature, the grandson of "Star-Spangled Banner" author Francis Scott Key, and even a sitting Illinois Democratic Congressman, followed by military suppression of rabidly partisan newspapers, including *The Chicago Times.* If he hadn't done that at the outset, the government would have gone to pieces, with Maryland and Washington lost to the Confederacy. But the suppression of *The Chicago Times* had incited protests by 40,000 Democrats in Chicago, contributing to the heavy defeat his party suffered in the 1862 elections.

My political enemies want to goad me into suppressing them, so they may go before the people between now and the election alleging that I am a tyrant with no respect for the Constitution, and that a Union governed by those means is not worth preserving.

He picked up his cherished copy of his favorite political cartoon, painted by the only popular artist who seemed friendly, of him trying to slay "The Dragon of Rebellion" while the Democratic Party Machine operating out of New York City, that voted two-to-one against him in 1860, chained him to an immovable "Constitution" anchored in stone:

The Rebellion must be crush'd but only constitutionally

He often responded to these allegations of subverting the Constitution by saying that when the existence of the government was threatened by rebellion, the Constitution must be interpreted broadly:

Is it possible to lose the nation and yet preserve the Constitution? By general law, life and limb must be protected, yet often a limb must be amputated to save a life; but a life is never wisely given to save a limb. I felt that measures otherwise unconstitutional might become lawful by becoming indispensable to the preservation of the Constitution through the preservation of the nation. Right or wrong, I assumed this ground and now avow it --- that I should not permit the wreck of government, country, and Constitution all together.

In extreme circumstances, he vowed to do so again, but this did not seem to be one. He decided to thank Governor Yates for his vigilance, telling him that while the incitements of *The Chicago Times* were severe, he did not now feel that suppressing the paper would improve the chances of himself, Yates, and all other Republican candidates prevailing in the upcoming election.

The next courier-delivered letter was from Charles D. Robinson, a Union Democrat, who published a newspaper in Green Bay, Wisconsin. He'd enlisted at the beginning of the war, hand fought from Bull Run to Fredericksburg, then was discharged with a crippling disease. He'd proven his patriotism beyond all doubt. Now he wanted the war to end before any more men were killed and crippled.

Union Democrats like him were inclined to vote for Mr. Lincoln's Republicans, but only if the war was purposed to restore the national authority over the seceded states. To them, that meant refraining from disfranchising the Democratic Party in the South, arresting boisterous anti-Lincoln Democrats in the North, or insisting that slavery must be abolished. Robinson advised Lincoln to rescind the Emancipation Proclamation, hoping to induce the Rebels to abandon the war and come back to the Union, slaves and all.

Lincoln knew how he felt, because he'd once felt that way --- that most Southerners were Union men at heart who'd been misled by hot-headed Secessionists. Don't rile them with talk about ending slavery, and they'd return to the Union when they knew the military arm of their rebellion was defeated.

He'd estimated correctly about men in the upper tier of Southern slave states of Delaware, Maryland, West Virginia, Kentucky, and Missouri. If he'd acted as precipitately in liberating slaves as the Radicals in his party wanted, he'd have lost those states to the Confederates in 1862. With those gone, the Union would be dissolved.

But he'd been wrong in appraising the motives of men in the Confederate heartland further south. Except for a very few like Andrew Johnson of Tennessee, who he'd asked to join his ticket as Vice President, most had transferred their loyalty to the Confederacy and could not be shaken from it. After all, it was he, not Jefferson Davis, who had just written a memorandum of "exceedingly probable" defeat in the next election. He needed to keep Union Democrats like Robinson on his side, while discouraging them from talking of rescinding the Emancipation Proclamation. He answered Robinson's letter:

I said in 1862: "If I could save the Union without freeing any slave, I would do it; and if I could save it by freeing all the slaves, I would do it; and if I could save it by freeing some, and leaving others alone, I would also do that. What I do about slavery and the colored race, I do because I believe it helps to save the Union; and what I forebear, I forbear because I do not believe it would help to save the Union; I shall do less whenever I shall believe what I am doing hurts the cause; and I shall do more whenever I shall believe doing more will help the cause."

I later wrote: "But Negroes, like other people, act upon motive. Why should they do anything for us if we will do nothing for them? If they stake their lives for us, they must be prompted by the strongest motive --- even the promise of freedom. And the promise, being made, must be kept." I am sure you will not, on due reflection, say that the promise being made, must be broken at the first opportunity.

If Jefferson Davis wishes, for himself, or for the benefit of his friends at the North, to know what I would do if he were to offer peace and re-union, saying nothing about slavery, let him try me.

He set that letter inside the copy book.

The last of the courier-delivered letters was from Henry Raymond, the editor of the Republican-aligned *New York Times*. As the elected chairman of the Republican National Committee, he would have a large say in deciding whether Mr. Lincoln would be nominated for a second term:

To His Excellency The President,

 I feel compelled to drop you a line concerning the political condition of the country as it strikes me. I am in active correspondence with your staunchest friends in every state and form them all I hear but report. The tide is setting strongly against them. Hon. E. B. Washburne writes that if an election were held now Illinois we should be beaten.

 Mr. Cameron writes that Pennsylvania is against us. Gov. Morton of Indiana writes that *nothing*, but the most strenuous efforts can carry Indiana.

 This state of New York, according to the best information I can get, would go 50,000 against us to-morrow. Nothing but the most resolute and decided action on the part of the government and its friends, can save the country from falling into hostile hands.

 Why would it not be wise, under these circumstances, to appoint a Commissioner, in due form, to make distinct proffers of peace to Jefferson Davis on the sole condition of acknowledging the supremacy of the Constitution, all other questions to be settled in a convention of the people of all the States?

 If it should be rejected, (as it would be,), it would plant seeds of disaffection in the South, dispel all the delusions about peace that prevail in the North, silence the clamors & damaging falsehoods of the opposition, reconcile public sentiment to the War, the draft, & the tax as inevitable necessities, and unite the North as nothing since firing on Fort Sumter has hitherto done.

 Very truly yours,
 Henry J. Raymond

I feel compelled to drop you a line concerning the political condition of the country as it strikes me. I am in active correspondence with your staunchest friends in every state and from them all I hear but one report. The tide is setting strongly against us. Hon. E. B. Washburne writes that were an election to be held now in Illinois we should be beaten.

Mr. Cameron writes that Pennsylvania is against us. Gov. Morton of Indiana writes that nothing but the most strenuous efforts can carry Indiana.

This state of New York, according to the best information I can get, would go 50,000 against us to-morrow. Nothing but the most resolute and decided action on the part of the government and its friends, can save the country from falling into hostile hands.

Why would it not be wise, under these circumstances, to appoint a Commissioner, in due form, to make distinct proffers of peace to Jefferson Davis on the sole condition of acknowledging the supremacy of the Constitution, *all other questions to be settled in a convention of the people of all the States?*

If it should be rejected, (as it would be,) it would plant seeds of disaffection in the South, dispel all the delusions about peace that prevail in the North, silence the clamors & damaging falsehoods of the opposition, reconcile public sentiment to the War, the draft, & the tax as inevitable necessities, and unite the North as nothing since firing on Fort Sumter has hitherto done.

Raymond's proposal sounded plausible. Jefferson Davis, for all his faults, did not try to deceive anybody into thinking he would voluntarily return to the Union under any circumstances. His rejection of compromise might take the wind out of the sails of Northern men who believed, or pretended to believe, that the South wanted to return to the Union if assurances were made that it could retain slavery.

On the other hand, Copperhead Peace Democrats would try to misrepresent it as an admission by Lincoln that the war was lost --- that he knew he couldn't beat the Confederates and was therefore sending a commissioner hat-in-hand to beg peace terms from Jeff Davis. That might harm his chances of re-election. He decided he'd bring up Raymond's letter for discussion at today's Cabinet meeting.

The Cabinet members lingered around the ice cabinet, some touching the exterior, then wiping their cool fingers across their sweaty brows. They sat down around the table in the corner of Mr. Lincoln's office. He began by passing around the sealed envelope containing his *Memorandum on the Probable Failure of Re-election*. He asked them to sign the back of the envelope without reading the document inside it.

"What's this mysterious document all about?" asked Secretary of War Stanton.

"Our marching orders after the election," answered Lincoln, with a lawyer's well-practiced aura of mystery. "I aim to open it the day after the election and read it to you then."

"Why can't we know what's in it now, before we sign it?" Stanton demanded.

"Because now is not the appropriate time," replied Lincoln, conjuring a playful demeanor. "I want you to endorse it to remind me of what I must do, when the appropriate time comes. You all have seen the envelope, so that will discourage me from throwing it away if I feel compelled to ignore it after the election. I'll either have to produce it or listen to you pester me about it for the rest of this administration!"

"Aaaaahhhh!" exclaimed Stanton, shaking the envelope while trying to peer through it to see if he could discern anything the president had written. "I should have used this technique with my clients. Unfortunately, they insist on reading contracts before signing them."

After the envelope was endorsed by the Cabinet, Lincoln locked it away in the bottom drawer of his desk. He then read Henry Raymond's letter, giving the grim prognosis for re-election, and proposing to send a peace commissioner to Richmond. He asked their advice, starting with his Secretary of State William Seward, also from New York.

"I concur with Raymond's assessment," advised Seward. "Thurlow Weed says New York City is even more against us now than in 1860. We'd have lost the State if the Democrats hadn't divided their party. Now they're united behind McClellan."

"It's the damned Irish," insisted Treasury Secretary William Fessenden. "They don't like Negroes. They're afraid if we set them free in the South, they'll be up here the next day taking their jobs and associating with their women."

"They were serfs in Ireland," explained Seward. "Owned by their masters, like the land they worked. They're free men here, with opportunities to better themselves for the first time in their lives. They don't want to share that opportunity with Negroes. It's understandable even if it's wrong."

"Might it help if we took the Emancipation Proclamation off the table?" asked Attorney General Edward Bates, a Missouri Unionist Democrat. "That's what keeps the Rebels fighting more than anything else, besides stirring up anti-Negro resentment in parts of the North." He eyed Lincoln. "Make it known that if the Rebels lay down their arms and re-enter the Union before the election, they'll keep their slaves."

Lincoln paraphrased the reply he'd written for Charles D. Robinson.

Seward listened intently. "I presume you to mean that slaves already emancipated by the Proclamation, and especially those fighting for us, will never be re-enslaved," he surmised. "But that if the Confederates lay down their arms and re-enter the Union now, those who are still in bondage might remain so."

"If the Rebellion ceases now," affirmed Lincoln, "the courts might rule that the Emancipation Proclamation has ceased its operation, and that no slaves will thereafter be emancipated by it. But so long as I am president, no Negro who has been set free shall ever be re-enslaved."

"I believe you should send Mr. Raymond to Richmond to explain those terms to Jefferson Davis, emphasizing our offers of compensation for slaves already emancipated," recommended Postmaster Montgomery Blair, also from Missouri. "Let Davis know we'll compensate the slaveholders fairly. That might set him at ease about discussing a return to the Union."

"What do you think?" Lincoln asked Stanton

51

Stanton shrugged. "I'm inclined to believe Davis will respond as Raymond expects, by declining to re-enter the Union on any terms, but who can say? Confederate losses must be as difficult for their people to bear as our losses are for us. Maybe he'll discuss it with his friends and together they will decide to soften their position."

Lincoln turned to Seward, who had formed an unlikely friendship with Davis before the war. Seward had no affinity for Davis' politics but had warmed to him when Davis joined him in the Senate in 1858. When Davis was blinded with an excruciating eye infection, Seward came to his room every night for weeks, spending hours reading the days' Senate proceedings. Davis' wife remarked that no person in Washington had a higher Christian spirit.

"You know Jefferson Davis. Do you anticipate he'll have anything constructive to say to a peace commissioner?"

"I don't consider it likely," replied Seward. "He's very stubborn once his mind is set. But if there's one chance in a thousand that any good comes of it, then you should send him. We won't know until we try."

The other Cabinet officers nodded agreement.

"Then I will send him." He looked at Stanton. "What else do we need to discuss today? Is the War Department paying its bills?"

"We're making do," answered Stanton. "The 'greenbacks' are stable at 45 cents to the gold dollar. Not the highest vote of confidence in our government, but at least they have stopped depreciating. Our war contractors and our soldiers accept them without excessive complaint. Our chief deficiency is men. We're paying $400 bounties to induce the dregs to enlist. That doesn't leave us enough to pay the veterans. Some are in arrears six months' pay…"

"I hear about that almost every day," interjected Lincoln. "It's terribly hard on their families, having their men away, and no money coming into their houses. Can't we expedite their pay? War contractors are wealthy. Let them wait for their money. Our soldiers require it for their suffering families."

"We wouldn't have to pay extortionate bounties for new men if we had longer enlistments," suggested Stanton. "Have you considered extending the enlistments of the Hundred Days Men for the duration of the war? There are over eighty thousand. That's more than Lee's whole army. They fought better than we expected against Jubal Early. If we put them where Lee doesn't expect them --- maybe land them on the North Carolina Coast and march inland to Raleigh --- he would have to decide whether to abandon Virginia or North Carolina. The loss of either would break the Insurgents' backs."

"We certainly erred in not setting longer terms of enlistment," Lincoln admitted. "But having set them, I do not believe it practical to extend them. The Hundred Days Men are mostly middle-aged bankers and merchants who never counted on fighting in the field. If I asked them to extend their enlistments, I don't expect many would voluntarily do it. They'd go back home and say, 'Old Lincoln tried to hornswoggle us into going up to the front.' If I extended their enlistments without their consent, most would desert, then go home and say worse."

"I understand these objections," said Stanton. "But it's so much easier to put those men in the field while we have them, than to muster in new recruits. If we fail to extend their enlistments and go on to lose the election for want of progress in the war, then we've lost everything. If we were to throw them into a new army in North Carolina, we might win the war before the election."

"We'd still have to find experienced officers to lead them," objected Lincoln. "We're woefully short of competent officers in Grant's army. I think we should not strip his army to create another in North Carolina. Even if we could find officers, it would take weeks to get the men transported and supplied. We need their votes at home in November even more than we need them in the field."

Stanton sighed. "We didn't think some things through at the beginning of the war, did we? If we'd enlisted our men for the duration of the war, we wouldn't be paying bounties to get men of very inferior quality now."

"We underestimated the Rebs," admitted Lincoln. "We thought they'd fold in ninety days. They almost did in '62 when McClellan got within sight of Richmond. Then the Rebs trotted out General Lee, who scared him off, and again at Antietam, even after Mac whupped him. I thought they'd fold after Gettysburg and Vicksburg, but Lee spooked Meade and there was no pursuit."

He tapped his fingers on the table. "Danged if I didn't think they'd fold this year. Now we're mustering out our Hundred Days Men. 'We only need them for a hundred days, because we'll be in Richmond by then.' We never got to Richmond. Instead, the Rebs showed up on our doorstep."

"At least they were here to help us shoo those Rebels off our doorstep!" remarked the always-optimistic John Hay who'd been taking the notes.

"It was too close for comfort," replied Lincoln. "And they raised Cain in Pennsylvania. I haven't had any peace from those parts since they burned Chambersburg. If they'd had a little more imagination, they could've ridden on over to Gettysburg and mocked me from the very spot where I made my address!"

"That would have been embarrassing!" exclaimed Hay. From his slight smile Lincoln could tell he was both chagrined and amused by the prospect of Rebels returning to the site of the great battle they'd lost thirteen months ago and thumbing their noses at Lincoln.

Stanton gave Hay a stern look for digressing the agenda. He turned to Lincoln. "There's one more thing you need to know about. Yates and Morton are running the governments of Illinois and Indiana on their personal authority. They've asked me to allocate money from the War Department to fund general operations in their states, including paying judges and administrative salaries. If they don't get it, the civil governments in those states will cease. I'll need Treasury to print three million greenbacks to tide them over for the rest of the year, and issue them to the War Department without informing Congress."

Treasury Secretary Fessenden's eyes widened. He looked at Lincoln, then at Stanton. "If the Cause fails, we'll be covered with prosecutions."

"If the Cause fails," vowed Stanton, "I do not wish to live."

"If the Cause fails, I do not wish to live."

The Cabinet meeting ended shortly before one o'clock. Mr. Lincoln ate lunch alone in the kitchen. Mary was in her bed upstairs with a wet towel over her head. Tad was playing with toy soldiers on the portico, to the amusement of the solders from the 166th Ohio Regiment, camped on the lawn. They'd served their 100 Days manning the forts around Washington, enabling veterans to get back in the line, then gone out to fight General Early's men in the battle that saved Washington. They were waiting for the president to address them before they boarded the train to take them home.

At half-past-one, he went out to the portico. Tad was holding his Union flag and standing amidst his toy soldiers.

"I've won seven battles!" he shouted to the soldiers, who were enjoying the moment immensely.

"Which battles were those, general?" asked a soldier.

"It was the Seven Days' Battle!" replied Tad cleverly.

"Hooray for Gen-rul Lincoln!" shouted the men. Mr. Lincoln appeared and waved. He put his arm around Tad then raised his son's arm high. The cheers of the men rattled the White House windows. The meaning was clear:

A nation may be said to consist of its territory, its people, and its laws. The territory is the only part which is of certain durability. One generation passeth away and another generation cometh, but the earth abideth forever. Our generation must pass the blessings of this Union to those generations who will follow us.

He'd said that in his last Message to Congress, reminding Union-loyal Americans that the territory possessed by the United States comprised a considerable portion of the Earth's temperate lands, suited by climate and geography for the fulfillment of mankind's aspirations. Would it remain the beacon of liberty, progress, and prosperity its Founders had ordained? Would Tad and the progeny of all other American families grow up to pursue life, liberty, and happiness? Or would they live in a diminished republic under the shadow of conflict with a powerful slaveholding empire whose northern border along the Potomac was visible from this spot?

He'd told the people that the issue embraced more than just the fate of the United States. It presented to the whole family of man the question whether a constitutional republic --- a democracy of the people by the people --- could maintain its territorial integrity against its own domestic foes. Could a discontented portion of the people, too few in numbers to control the government, arbitrarily break it up? Was there in all republics this inherent fatal weakness? Must a government, of necessity, be too strong for the liberties of its own people, or too weak to maintain its own existence? If Americans dissolved their free republic by making war against themselves, would the destiny not only of the nation, but of all Mankind, be bent away from freedom and toward tyranny?

He was gratified by their cheering that these men grasped the importance of this moment. When their cheering stopped, their colonel called them to attention. He felt a tingling in his heart as he had on so many occasions when he spoke to friendly crowds. On those occasions his voice communicated more than words.

"Soldiers of the 166th Ohio: I am most happy to meet you on this occasion. I understand that it has been your honorable privilege to stand in the defense of your country, when your service was most required, and that now you are on your way to your families.

"Nowhere in the world is presented a government of so much liberty and equality. To the humblest and poorest amongst us are held out the highest privileges and positions. The present moment finds me at the White House, yet there is as good a chance for your children as there was for my father's.

"Again, I admonish you not to be turned from your stern purpose of defending your beloved country and its free institutions by any arguments urged by ambitious and designing men. Stand fast to the Union and the old flag. Soldiers I bid you God-speed to your homes."

"Hurrah!" shouted the men once more as they clicked their heels to attention. Their colonel allowed them to throw their hats into the air and break ranks to retrieve them. Lucky indeed was the man who went home with the same hat he'd been issued!

He waved farewell as the colonel called them to order and marched them down Pennsylvania Avenue toward the railroad depot. He envied these men. They'd done all their country asked of them. If the war failed, no one would blame them. No matter how it turned out, they'd have exciting stories to tell their families and friends and their children and grandchildren for the rest of their lives. They'd go back to their civilian roles as bankers, shopkeepers, clerks, and farmers, always remembering this moment of glory.

They would move through the years, perhaps finishing their lives in a distant place and time. The youngest would be living in the Twentieth Century by the time they reached Lincoln's present age. Would it be a time of peace, progress, and prosperity under the blessed government of a restored Union? Or a bitter time of recrimination for a dissolved nation because people in one section had valued their slaves more than the common destiny of a united country?

He was certain of one thing: that these men would never forget this day when they'd stood with their president and received his thanks for a duty well-performed. An uneasy question entered his mind:

What would these men think if they knew that I am planning to send a peace commissioner to meet with Jefferson Davis in Richmond? What will the men fighting in Virginia and Georgia think? Will they think the war is over, and that they are entitled to go home like these men here who have served their hundred days?

He escorted Tad back to his room and sat with him while he worked his additions and subtractions. He left when Tad's tutor returned to review the lessons. He looked in on Mary. "Are you all right, Mother?"

Mrs. Lincoln smiled. "Yes, thank you, Father. I am remembering what a wonderful husband I have. I know I do vex you too much. My expenses for the dresses were inexcusable..."

He held her hand. "Don't concern yourself about it any further. You will make a fine impression at the public reception tomorrow night."

He returned to his office. Hay, Nicolay, and Stoddard were sorting out the morning's correspondence he'd left them. Stoddard was working the copy press while Nicolay and Hay wrote replies to the letters the president had delegated them to answer at their discretion. He enjoyed watching them work. Without them, the demands of the office would have crushed him. *I have risen high in life, to have **three** secretaries!*

He sat down at his desk and proceeded to write his response to Henry Raymond. Perhaps it would be remembered as his most crucial letter of the war. It always took longer to write these letters than he'd anticipated. He had to start this one over after poorly stating his point in the second paragraph. He had to get up after each paragraph and banter with his secretaries to relax his cramped hand and his tiring mind. His mechanically inventive mind recalled the patent he'd received in 1849 for an air pump to lift steamboats over sandbars. Perhaps after the war he would have time to think about inventing a printing press easily used by persons in their homes and offices.

How wonderful it would be to have a personal printing press, where each pull of a lever would produce the clear imprint of a letter on paper. That would be an invention equivalent to photography and the telegraph. If we can get past this war, we will move on to a new world of invention. In a generation or two the Rebels will not need slaves to work their farms. Horse-drawn machinery will do the work of twenty men. Steam power might do the work of a hundred. They don't know they are fighting to remain part of a vanishing past.

He finished his reply to Henry Raymond at a quarter-past-four:

Executive Mansion,

Washington August 23, 1864.

Sir,

You will proceed forthwith and obtain, if possible, a conference for peace with Hon. Jefferson Davis, or any person by him authorized for that purpose.

You will address him in entirely respectful terms, at all events, and in any that may be indispensable to secure the conference.

At said conference you will propose, on behalf of this government, that upon the restoration of the Union and the national authority, the war shall cease at once. All remaining questions to be left for adjustment by peaceful modes. If this be accepted, hostilities to cease at once.

If it be not accepted, you will then request to be informed what terms, if any, embracing the restoration of the Union, would be accepted. If any such be presented you in answer, you will forthwith report the same to this government, and await further instructions.

If the presentation of any terms embracing the restoration of the Union be declined, you will then request to be informed what terms of peace would be accepted; and on receiving any answer, report the same to this government, and await further instructions.

A. Lincoln

You will proceed forthwith and obtain, if possible, a conference for peace with Hon. Jefferson Davis, or any person by him authorized for that purpose.

You will address him in entirely respectful terms, at all events, and in any that may be indispensable to secure the conference.

At said conference you will propose, on behalf of this government, that upon the restoration of the Union and the national authority, the war shall cease at once. All remaining questions to be left for adjustment by peaceful modes. If this be accepted, hostilities to cease at once.

If it be not accepted, you will then request to be informed what terms, if any embracing the restoration of the Union, would be accepted. If any such be presented you in answer, you will forthwith report the same to this government, and await further instructions.

If the presentation of any terms embracing the restoration of the Union be declined, you will then request to be informed what terms of peace would be accepted; and on receiving any answer, report the same to this government, and await further instructions.

At 4:27 Mary, who was supervising the cooks in the kitchen, walked to open the door on the far side of his office and called him.

"Frederick Douglass is here to see you!"

Exactly on time, as always. The mark of a disciplined man.

He decided he needed to read the letter one more time before he asked one of his secretaries to deliver it personally to Henry Raymond in New York.

"Is it dark in here or is it just me?" asked Frederick Douglass when Lincoln greeted him in the Red Room. He strained his eyes to see in the unusually dim light.

Lincoln laughed. "It *is* dark, and it's not just you!" He looked out the window. A squall was blowing in from the Chesapeake. Rain began spattering the windows, followed by gusts of wind. He called for the butler Peter Brown, a free Negro, to light the lamps.

"Thank you, Mr. President," said Douglass. "You know, at my age it's becoming difficult enough to see even in broad daylight."

Mrs. Lincoln directed the cooks to put out hot tea and cold tea. Douglass, who'd spent a year and a half lecturing against slavery in England and Ireland, drank his tea hot in the British style with cream and sugar, while Lincoln enjoyed his chilled with mint. Mary greeted Douglass with a smile and shook his hand.

"Welcome to our home, Mr. Douglass. Time is so scarce during war. These moments with our friends are treasured."

Most Whites showed disdain when they met him, as if they were greeting a mad bull. He thought the Lincolns to be so secure in themselves that they did not need to feel superior to Negroes to think well of themselves as white people. Would the day ever come when most white people acted that way?

The president and Douglass sat down and exchanged small talk about their families, especially the progress of their children. After a few minutes Douglass got to the point of his visit.

"Mr. President, I have heard that you intend to send peace commissioners to Richmond to talk to Jefferson Davis."

"May I ask the source of this information?"

"Horace Greeley. His information has always been reliable."

Lincoln surmised that Henry Raymond had talked to Greeley who owned *The New York Tribune*. Raymond and Greeley were rival newspaper editors who didn't always see eye-to-eye, but they agreed the Union must be preserved, and that to save the Union peace must be discussed with the Confederates.

"Yes, it's true," Lincoln confirmed. "I intend to send a peace commissioner to Richmond to discover on what, if any, terms Jefferson Davis will command his armies to lay down their arms, and his people to return peaceably to the Union. I expect he'll say reunion is not possible on any terms. Then the people, North and South, will know we have offered fair terms in good faith for restoring peace and have been refused. Please don't let this conversation leave this room."

"Your motives are worthy," replied Douglass. "But you can't be sure how Davis will respond. What if he says he'll discuss peace with McClellan after the election? Those two were like father and son before the war. If the people think they will have peace with McClellan, they will elect him, without caring about the particulars. Davis can say he'll accept an armistice now in return for some vague promise to re-enter the Union later. If word of that gets out, our armies will disperse."

Lincoln sipped his tea, then replied: "If we lose the election because too many voters in the North believe I have not sought peace when it could have been obtained, then the South will gain its independence. The Union will be dissolved, and slavery will continue indefinitely."

Douglass had anticipated that reply. "In that case, slavery will only poison the Rebel States. It will poison the land on which it now resides but will spread no further. If you conclude the war by allowing the South to reenter the Union with slavery, the Rebellion will infect the Union in living form forever. The slaveowners will resume their work of spreading it far and wide in the Western Territories. After bringing these into the Union as new Slave States, they will demand the annexation of Mexico and Cuba. You must conquer the Rebellion now, eliminating every vestige of slavery by pointing our guns at the slaveholders and

68

forcing them to release their slaves. There must be no questions about the Free States ending the war on our terms."

Lincoln considered the point.

"Think about who might follow you into this office," conjectured Douglass. "When I met Andrew Johnson, he snorted as if I were a wild buffalo. If you are re-elected, he will become your vice president. If, God forbid, anything happens to you, Negroes will have no friends in this White House."

"Well, that's something to think about," confessed Lincoln. "Few men live as long as they calculate."

"There is one thing more," said Douglass, raising his hand for emphasis. "Why is it that Negroes are always last to be considered in discussions about what is right for this country? Last year you proposed to liberate us, then ship us off to Africa and South America. At the same time, Congress passed the Homestead Act granting free lands in the West to white people and foreigners, but not a single acre for Negroes, including those fighting to save the Union. Our reward was to be expelled to some barren country in the tropics. At least masters feed their slaves. We would die of starvation and disease if some future president and Congress decides to expel us from this country."

A flush of red showed through Douglass' chocolate-dark complexion. Lincoln sought to defuse his anger before it exploded.

"I thought I had made it clear that we were not seeking to encourage Negroes to emigrate because of any deficiency in your race, but rather because of the deficiency in Whites to accept you as equals," Lincoln explained. "I had thought you'd be happier in a country governed by your own people."

Douglass closed his eyes and tried to compose himself.

"Mr. President, *this* is our country. We know no other. We are Africans no more. My father was a white overseer. I am as much white as black. All of me is American. We are perfectly content to pursue our rights to life, liberty, and happiness here. All we ask is that you allow us the same freedoms that Whites possess. Allow us access to the ballot and the courts, and the right to work for wages, and own businesses and property. Allow us the same rights to prosper in this country as Whites, and we will take care of the rest. All we ask is that your government shall interpret the Constitution to conform to the spirit of the American Revolution: '*All* men are created equal!'"

Lincoln sighed. "If I have been slow in acknowledging Negroes as citizens equal in constitutional rights to Whites, it is only because I thought it best to win the war now and pursue Negro equality later."

"*That* is the problem!" exclaimed Douglass, his voice rising. "That's exactly it! When it comes to applying the Constitution to Negroes, the answer is always 'later.' George Washington and Thomas Jefferson proposed that the first Congress should abolish slavery. They came within a single vote of abolishing it. They didn't get that last vote because somebody said, 'Not now. It will be easier to abolish slavery later.' So, slavery was spread over the entire South! Then the North and South agreed to limit it according to the Missouri Compromise. Then when the Slave States gained the votes of Northern Democrats, they repealed the Missouri Compromise, and slavery was allowed to spread throughout the free territories of the West. Then came the *Dred Scott Decision* inviting it to infect the Free States of the North."

"That was Stephen Douglas's and Judge Taney's doing," Lincoln insisted. "Douglas is deceased, and Taney looks like he won't live out the year. When he passes, I'll appoint one of our people to the Supreme Court. Times are changing."

"Are they really? Douglas and Taney perpetuated slavery because so many people, including here in the North, kept running away from the founding principle of this country, that *all* men are created equal. 'We will honor the principle *later*,' they say. 'Just give us a little more time to continue denying the Negro the right to eat the bread that his labor earns.' Evil always begets more evil, Mr. President. Don't believe it will be easier to fight it later. It never is."

Lincoln started to speak, but Douglass was not finished.

"Do you want to know why this war is so hard? It's because men who love freedom are wondering what it's all about. You seek peace by returning to the embrace of the Confederates? They've never pretended to believe that men of color were created equal. They are not hypocrites like so many in the North! If the Confederates were to come back into the Union with slavery intact, it wouldn't take a single day for white men at the North and South to start congratulating each other on how they were able to save the country without freeing the Negroes! Stop fighting this war to serve only White interests. Start fighting for freedom for all men, and then we'll win it together!"

Lincoln nodded. "Will you be staying with us tonight? We could discuss this further."

Douglass decided it would be best not to press him any further. He'd given Mr. Lincoln enough points to consider. He would reach his decision without requiring any more information.

"Thank you, Mr. President, you are most gracious. But I must catch the seven o'clock train. I need to be in Boston in time for my meeting with Mr. Garrison tomorrow." William Lloyd Garrison was Douglass' partner in the Abolitionist press. Mr. Lincoln walked him to the door and called Mary to say farewell.

Douglass took Mary's hand. Few Whites, and especially not Southern Whites, would allow a black man to touch them. Mary did not flinch. Lincoln went back to the Red Room to finish his tea. Just before six o'clock, Peter Brown came in to announce the presence of General Lew Wallace.

6:00 PM: General Lew Wallace

"Mary, allow me to present General Lew Wallace," said Mr. Lincoln. "They say he couldn't find the Rebels at Shiloh, but he didn't have a bit of trouble finding them here, did you General? I tender you my thanks for saving the city."

"It was impossible *not* to find them, sir. Everyone knew they were headed directly for Washington."

Wallace was made the official scapegoat of the Federal near-disaster during the first day's battle at Shiloh. In truth, Generals Grant and Sherman brought on the debacle by failing to post pickets to alert them of the Confederate approach. When the Confederates struck without warning, Grant issued confusing orders sending Wallace's men marching away from the battle, then blamed him for being out of position.

He was relieved from active duty and sent to backwater commands for the duration of the war. The war had nevertheless found him. He'd been in command of state militias at Cincinnati in September 1862 when the Confederates' Kentucky offensive broke through to the Ohio River. He'd organized his men superbly, turning the Confederates away. He'd been furloughed home to Southern Indiana in summer 1863 when Confederate raider John Hunt Morgan had raced across Indiana and Ohio. He'd successfully defended railroad junctions with ad hoc forces that slowed Morgan enough to enable Northern forces to blunt his raid and later capture him.

Most recently he'd been shunted into another backwater at Baltimore, far behind the front --- until Jubal Early's Corps came rampaging up past Washington. As soon as he had learned of Early's approach, he marched his brigade of Hundred Days militiamen out of Baltimore and posted them astride the road leading into Washington.

There Wallace's inexperienced men fought Early's battle-hardened veterans. Though defeated, they'd fought well, inflicting significant losses on the Confederates and halting them for a day. General Grant had time to transfer two corps of veterans from the siege lines around Richmond to the Washington defenses just as Early was forming up an assault to capture the city.

Wallace was belatedly recognized as the hero who'd saved Washington. Even so, he maintained a dour disposition, as if his battle that saved Washington had failed to redeem his reputation tarnished at Shiloh. Mr. Lincoln, wanting to acknowledge his valor, had asked Mary to make him feel appreciated.

She winked at Wallace. "Thank you, General, for stopping those Rebels," she said playfully. "I would not have wanted to be hosting Confederates for dinner. I much prefer the present company."

"You see there, General," Mr. Lincoln assured him, "how important your action was! If you had not fought the Rebels outside of town, I do believe they would have captured this city. That would have cheered them beyond all measure. It would have returned thousands of shirkers to their ranks and restored their faith in victory. They believe they will always receive a miracle to keep their cause alive. If not for you, Jubal Early just might have given them one."

He presented Wallace a letter of commendation just received from General Grant:

Head Quarters Armies of the United States,

If Early had been but one day earlier, he might have entered the capital before the arrival of the reinforcements I had & sent. General Wallace contributed on this occasion by the defeat of the troops under him, a greater benefit to the cause than often falls to the lot of a commander of an equal force to render by means of a victory.

Yours respectfully,
Lt. Gen. U. S. Grant

If Early had been but one day earlier, he might have entered the capital before the arrival of the reinforcements I had sent. General Wallace contributed on this occasion by the defeat of the troops under him, a greater benefit to the cause than often falls to the lot of a commander of an equal force to render by means of a victory.

Yours respectfully, Lt. Gen. U.S. Grant

Wallace read the letter and smiled. "I am honored to have been in the right place to serve my country when it needed me."

"And I am pleased that General Grant has recognized your contribution. It took a while, but war is nothing if not confusion. It takes time to sort things out. Well, let's talk about it over dinner."

Dinner was informal. When each dish was placed on the table Lincoln picked it up, asking who would "like a helping," and ladling it into the plates. The Lincolns asked about Wallace's family and his plans after the war. Wallace said he would like to study theology and write about it.

"I expect you already know a thing or two about theology, general," suggested Lincoln. "At least the part that involves faith. I imagine that being relieved of command after Shiloh was harsh medicine. Many officers would have resigned from the army and gone home. But you continued to serve our cause faithfully. Because you did, you likely prevented the Rebels from capturing this city. You will be remembered because you placed the country's interests before your own."

"I was angry at being blamed for the first day's retreat," admitted Wallace, "But I understood that the country is larger than me. I kept remembering the words of Nathan Hale: 'My only regret is that I have but one life to give for my country.' My service is small compared to others who have given their lives. If all my country asked of me was to serve it in a quiet theater, so someone else could command at the front, then I was proud to do that."

"Oh, how you have cheered, and warmed my heart!" exclaimed Lincoln. "Much of my time is taken up with people who put their own interests first, before everything else. Chief among them are officers who want me to authorize courts of inquiry against other officers who they feel have slighted them in some way. It has taken a long time for men like you to rise to the top. Finally, we have you where we need you. Now it is up to me to find a way to win the election, so the war can continue until the Rebellion is defeated."

"I am certain you will be re-elected," Wallace assured him, "because people know you are working for a cause larger than yourself. They know that your only concern is to reunite the country in a just way, and that you care nothing for yourself. My study of theology leads me to believe that selfless devotion to a righteous cause is powerful, Mr. President. It is more powerful than you may know."

Lincoln raised his finger. "That touches on something I have often wondered about: why God appears so reticent to back our cause. By His power, he could give the victory to either side on any day. Yet the contest proceeds, with great misery and loss of life, and seemingly without advantage to either side."

"I suppose that if He wanted to solve our disputes for us, He would have done so long before the war ever started," suggested Wallace. "Men of bad faith on both sides of the Ohio got us into this war. Men of good faith on both sides are doing the best they know how to end the war on terms they consider just. Perhaps He figures that since so many men had a hand in starting the war, it will take the hands of many to finish it."

Lincoln nodded to show he was impressed by Wallace's reasoning.

"That's a well-considered view of it, general. I have tried to maintain my faith in the rightness of our cause, and in the ability of the loyal people to understand it and see it through to victory. I have seen some very dark days since taking this office. I think the darkest was after our defeat at Fredericksburg. I had just issued the Emancipation Proclamation. I believed Providence would bless our cause with victory. Instead, we suffered the most severe defeat of the war. Yet, the hands have been there to recover us from those defeats and to keep fighting the Rebels. Alas, they don't seem any more inclined to give up their Rebellion now than they did three years ago."

"Defeats in a just cause should increase our faith and induce us to correct our errors," insisted Wallace. "Without defeats, there could be no faith, could there? Maybe that is what is taking so much time --- to so thoroughly defeat the Rebels that they will never again think of slavery and insurrection. I just hope they will not continue to make trouble for us after we have brought them back into our country."

Mr. Lincoln raised his head, as he was prone to doing, when considering a profound point. The thought came to him: *How canst thou appreciate the calm, if thou hast not passed through the tempest?* He didn't remember if the verse was stated in the Bible in exactly that way, but it was the theme of many stories he remembered from his self-taught days of reading The Good Book.

"They are a pragmatic people," he surmised. "I believe they will make as good citizens as any when they are no longer distracted by arguments for secession and slavery. Without slavery, and all the interests that surround it, the South will become more prosperous than it could ever have become with slavery as its foundation. The South won't have to waste its productive energies guarding against slave revolts. It will develop its commerce with free labor to a degree its people cannot now imagine. Whites and Negroes will prosper together. The North will prosper by trading with a prosperous South. We will become a new country, united by freedom and prosperity for all."

Mary returned from the kitchen and sat down. "I wish my sisters in the South could hear you!" She turned toward Wallace. "Their husbands are Confederate officers! They would kill my husband and destroy the government if they could. I hope they get killed first."

Her harsh words surprised Wallace. He had heard the nasty rumors about Mary being a Confederate spy. Hearing her speak her true views left no doubt that she was loyal to her husband and the Union with all her body, heart, and soul.

Mr. Lincoln put his hand gently on his wife's. "They'll be all right," he counseled. "We must have faith, not only in the justice of our cause, but also in the rehabilitation of our enemies when they are defeated. That is difficult, I know, but it is what our Savior said we must do. We must also have faith that the slaves, when freed, will prosper under our Constitution, like all other people. We must have faith that slave owners, and those they led into this wicked Rebellion, will recognize their errors, and to understand, as General Wallace does, that the country is larger than any person."

"That is why you will be re-elected," insisted Wallace. "Because you have faith in things beyond yourself. I know McClellan. He is a good man, but one who only has faith in himself. He thinks that only he can end the war on fair terms. A man who thinks only of himself may go far but will not succeed in the greatest things. McClellan did not win the war on the field, and he cannot win it if elected president. Most people will understand that. They will place their faith in you."

Mr. Lincoln had a sudden insight that the end of the war might be nearer than he'd thought.

"If we win this election, then we will win the war," he predicted. "The Confederates look strong on the outside, but they are burning themselves up from the inside out, like a hollow log that catches fire from the center. Some Insurgent leaders are proposing to conscript Negro slaves into their armies. They are truly hollowed out if they are asking those who they considered fit only for servitude to fight for them. Their last hope is that we, the Loyal People, will falter. We will shatter that last hope if the Union Party prevails in the election. Thanks to our people with faith like you, general. After what you have told me tonight, I am convinced we will prevail!"

With that, the dinner broke up on a happy note. The Lincolns bid General Wallace good night. Mrs. Lincoln supervised the cleaning up by the staff of the dining room and kitchen while Mr. Lincoln carried a hot coffee to the Red Room, whose beauty and expansive view of the Potomac inspired him. He needed to rest before going to his office to finish his letter to Henry Raymond. He sipped his hot coffee while the golden rays of the sun touched the tops of the green trees and lit the brown waters of the Potomac. On the other side of the river, about a mile away, was the Rebel State of Virginia.

I lost my young friend Elmer Ellsworth, the bright shining star of youth, killed within sight of here, on the first day of hostilities. Edward Baker, my dearest lifelong friend, and godfather of my dearest Eddie, was killed at Balls Bluff also within sight of that river. It has become a river of death for me.

But isn't that also true for near a million families? A thousand men a day, and more, are being killed or crippled in the battles around Richmond, and more in Georgia and other places.

They say that before the war, it was a three-and-a-half-hour train ride from here to Richmond. Now it has been three and a half years of fighting, and we are still not there. The Rebels are vowing to fight for twenty more years, if necessary, until the next generation rises to take the place of the fallen. The Heavens are draped in black, and the Rebels vow that the war has only just begun.

We must finish this war. If we do not, other wars will loom. We will have wars for the Eastern Shore of the Chesapeake; wars for Kentucky and Missouri; wars for New Mexico and California; wars for Colorado and Utah. And wars in Mexico, Cuba, and Central America as the Confederates try to expand their slave empire. We must finish this war now, or we will be fighting it eternally.

He eased back and stretched out his long body on the comfortable chair and footstool. He dozed.

7:45 PM: Rainbow and Lightning

He was aroused by a booming rumble from the South. For a moment, he dreamed it was another Confederate attack. Then he realized it was the air-moving rumble of thunder. He went outside to make sure. He walked across the corner of the White House front yard and peered around the Treasury Building for an unobstructed view of the sky. These days he was accompanied by a bodyguard of three whenever he left the White House. A week and a half ago he'd been shot through his hat while riding out alone at night to the Soldiers' Home three miles north of town, the home for elderly and disabled soldiers. He enjoyed their comradery, as well as the cooler air on the hilltop, where he slept in a stone guest cottage on these hot nights.

He never found out who fired that shot, or why. He surmised it was a nervous homeowner firing out into the night to ward off a possible intruder, or perhaps discharging the rifle carelessly at the end of a hunt. Could it have been an assassination attempt? It was unlikely the shooter would have known he'd be coming that way at that time --- or could see him in the darkness. At any rate, Stanton had forbidden him from travelling alone anymore. The bodyguard assigned from a Pennsylvania regiment flanked him right, left, and rear. It reminded him of the visible and invisible threats to his life, and about what Frederick Douglass had said about who would follow him in the White House. Life was fragile. He might pass sooner than he thought. Didn't everybody?

I must do what I know to be necessary each day, because God guarantees no man a tomorrow.

He passed other soldiers, who waved and cheered. They were from another Ohio regiment of Hundred Days Men who'd pitched their tents on the White House grounds because they were going home. He was scheduled to address them tomorrow, as he'd addressed the regiment today. Time seemed to fly by these days. This afternoon's address already seemed far in the past.

He passed around the side of the Treasury Building where the lamps were starting to shine through the windows as the sun touched the horizon. The night staff would be printing greenbacks and answering correspondence until the sun came up.

As soon as he cleared the edge of the building, he saw a thundercloud stretching upward for miles into the sky, drizzling a misty rain from its bottom. A rainbow, backlit by the setting sun, shone through the mist. Suddenly a shaft of lighting arced through the rainbow and streaked overhead, reaching for the blue sky to the north.

The thunder and lightning of war overarched by a glorious rainbow of peace!

A fresh wind blew in from the north, with a scent of rain and the first cool hint of autumn. In that instant, he glimpsed a vision of the future beyond the war. Was this an omen that the "rainbow of peace" would follow the thunder and lightning and war, would encompass the entire United States, and all its people, North and South, black and white?

8:30 PM: The Work of Dusk

He returned to the White House as dusk fell. Mary had finished her work downstairs and retired to her bedroom. As soon as Tad heard him come up the steps, he grabbed some toys off the floor in his room and came running into his father's office. Mr. Lincoln hugged him. He asked about Tad's new toys --- a carved horse, and figurines of Indians and frontiersmen. He sat down to finish his letter to Henry Raymond, while Tad played on the carpet. He pulled the letter out of his locked bottom drawer and begin reading it again:

He paused. Something no longer seemed right. Maybe it was the warning from Frederick Douglass that if the public learned he was talking to Jefferson Davis, the armies would disperse, and the Rebels would feel they'd won the war. If they returned to the Union, it would only be because they believed they'd "taught the Damn Yankees a lesson not to interfere with our ownership of slaves."

There were also Lew Wallace's words about faith. Did he have so little faith in victory that he'd send a peace commissioner to Richmond to talk to Jefferson Davis knowing no possible good would come from it? He recalled the stirring words of Secretary of War Stanton. *"If the cause fails, I do not wish to live."*

Now that was faith! Stanton, along with governors Yates and Morton, was risking prosecution and incarceration for spending government money without authorization from Congress. If McClellan prevailed in November, not only Stanton but also Yates, Morton, Fessenden, and possibly himself, could face indictment and trial. That risk had not deterred any of them from doing what they felt they must do to save the Union. His conversation with Lew Wallace made him think of another memorandum he'd written to himself nearly two years ago.

He took a key out of the top drawer and unlocked the bottommost drawer where he kept his most confidential papers. He pulled out the only other letter he'd written to himself, that he called his ***Meditation on the Divine Will***. He'd written it nearly two years ago in September 1862 in what in retrospect seemed the distant morning of the war. Both sides knew the sun must soon set on a war bleeding Americans beyond their endurance, so they were talking about peace, but each unwilling to make the concessions to end it on the other side's terms. The war was stalemated now as then, with blood soaking the land every day, from the lives of hundreds, and sometimes thousands, of America's best young men snuffed out in their primes. Was he really doing God's will in continuing to prosecute the war to preserve the authority of the Union Government over the full extent of its former territory? He was comforted by the ***Meditation i***n times like these when his faith was most severely tested:

September 22, 1862

The will of God prevails. In great contests each party claims to act in accordance with the will of God. Both may be, and one must be, wrong. God cannot be for and against the same thing at the same time.

In the present <u>Civil War</u> it is quite possible that God's purpose is something different from the purpose of either party — and yet the human instrumentalities, working just as they do, are of the best adaptation to <u>effect</u> His purpose. I am almost ready to say that this is probably true — that God wills this contest, and wills that it shall not end yet.

By his mere great power, on the minds of the now contestants, he could have either saved or destroyed the Union without a human contest. Yet the contest began. And, having begun, He could give the final victory to either side any day. Yet the contest proceeds.

A. Lincoln

The will of God prevails. In great contests each party claims to act in accordance with the will of God. Both may be, and one must be, wrong. God cannot be for and against the same thing at the same time.

In the present Civil War it is quite possible that God's purpose is something different from the purpose of either party -- and yet the human instrumentalities, working just as they do, are of the best adaptation to effect His purpose. I am almost ready to say that this is probably true -- that God wills this contest, and wills that it shall not end yet.

By his mere great power, on the minds of the now contestants, he could have either saved or destroyed the Union without a human contest. Yet the contest began. And, having begun, He could give the final victory to either side any day. Yet the contest proceeds.

He contemplated:

Why is Providence so reticent to bless our cause? I thought I was doing His will by signing the Emancipation Proclamation in September 1862, after He blessed us with victory at Antietam. No sooner had I signed it than the blessings stopped, like a well run dry. The Copperheads put some our best Union men out of office in the 1862 elections, then the Rebels slaughtered our men at Fredericksburg and humiliated most severely at Chancellorsville. We balanced the scales at Vicksburg and Gettysburg, but no more than that; and now stuck again, with losses most severe, and the patience of the people so thin, and with so little progress forward. The way the war is going, the Confederates have as much right to claim the blessings of Providence as we do.

Providence seemed indifferent in so many things! It hadn't shielded his two young sons Eddie and Willie from death in childhood. It hadn't shielded his two best friends, Elmer Ellsworth and Senator Edward Baker, for whom dearest departed Eddie was named, from death in combat. It hadn't dissuaded his favorite bother-in-law Ben Helm from fighting and dying for the Confederates Chickamauga. It hadn't provided his Union generals any insights to avoid leading their men into the slaughter pens at Balls Bluff, Fredericksburg, and Cold Harbor.

And yet, I, too, have been reticent in exercising my powers as Chief Executive. How many decisions do I make that people find incomprehensible?

Denying the request of those men from Andersonville to resume prisoner exchanges will cause thousands of our men to perish, very likely including them. I declined their request because I believed that decision was necessary to save the Union, and thereby to preserve the liberties for millions alive now and yet to be born.

I cannot explain my reasoning to them because that would be an admission that I fear resuming the prisoner exchanges would lose us the war, by putting more Rebels back in the field while inducing more of our men to surrender. The mere admission of this would have a detrimental, and perhaps fatal, effect on our Cause. Those five 'men of honor' must therefore proceed back to Andersonville, and very possibly to their deaths, when I have it in my power to accede to their request to resume the exchanges and save their lives and countless others.

But I have spared the life of the woman's husband, because his death would have been not only unjust, but also detrimental to prosecuting the war. Perhaps God, though infinitely mighty, is vexed by the same decisions of when to act, and when to refrain from acting, as are we mortals of His creation. He cannot reveal His reasons for allowing evil to afflict us any more than I can reveal my reasons for refusing to relieve those honor-bound men of their terrible duty to return to Andersonville.

Rather than becoming pensive in trying circumstances, he drew on his habit of recalling moments of humor. He remembered a group of preachers from Chicago who came to see him in 1862, to hector him to understand their view that God willed him to end slavery now. Remembering the debauchery lurking in the taverns, bordellos, and gambling dens of the raucous prairie metropolis, he'd told them: "If that is God's message, then He is sending it by a most circuitous route, by way of that wicked city of Chicago!"

Those stern preachers laughed uproariously, then listened respectfully while he pointed out his reasons for waiting until the proper time to liberate the slaves. He told them he must consider whether his actions would be constitutional and expedient. He said it would not be expedient to liberate the slaves when the Confederacy was fighting well, as that would be seen as an act of desperation that might drive Kentucky and Missouri into their ranks. Better to wait until a victory was won, so the liberation would be seen as a fruit of success. He waited until after the victory at Antietam to issue the Emancipation Proclamation.

The very next battle at Fredericksburg was the most severe Union defeat of the war. Union morale sagged and desertions soared but in defeat and in abhorrence by soldiers who would fight for the Union but not for the Negro. God had favored Emancipation in any immediately obvious way. Yet enough Union men continued to fight and when necessary to die,, and the Emancipation Proclamation began its work of liberating the slaves in each district of the Confederacy the Union armies entered. Even a few Confederate leaders now talked about freeing their slaves and arming them to fight for the Confederacy. If God's will was inscrutable, it nevertheless seemed to be working in the right direction.

If I must bide my time, as I did in waiting for the right time to issue the Emancipation Proclamation, then surely the Lord must bide His!

In the meantime, I must have faith in the things I can see. I must have faith in the cause of maintaining the precious government my predecessors bequeathed me. I must have faith in my officers and men, who are living and dying in extreme privation.

Above all else, I must have faith in the people. I went up to Gettysburg last October and told them that this war was being fought so that government of the people, by the people, and for the people would not perish. If I cannot trust the people to vote wisely, then there is no point in pretending that we are fighting for a "government of the people." We might as well impose a dictatorship and forego all pretense of caring what the people think.

I must have at least as much faith in leading the Union Loyal people to fight for freedom in a united country as the Rebel leaders have faith in their cause of breaking the Union to keep a third of their people enslaved.

I cannot deceive myself into believing Jefferson Davis will end the war on my terms of restoring the Union, when I know he has the faith to continue fighting it to end it on his terms of breaking it. If I send my representative to talk peace in his house, the people will rightly think me a faithless fool, and will abandon me and the National Cause I lead.

The people have chosen me to lead them through this fiery trial. I must have the faith of Frederick Douglass that freedom is God's desired destiny of all persons. I must have the faith of General Wallace, who cared nothing for himself, and everything for the country.

He decided against sending the letter to Raymond. He put it back in his bottom drawer upside down on top of his *Memorandum on Probable Failure of Re-election.* He placed his *Meditation on the Divine Will* face up on top of both, then locked the drawer. His work for this day was complete There would be no peace mission to Richmond.

He remained in his office reading the newspapers from New York --- Horace Greeley's *Tribune* and Henry Raymond's *Times* --- that one of his secretaries had left on his desk. Mary got up from her bed and brought in a puzzle. She and Tad began putting it together on the table in the corner, the one he and his Cabinet had gathered around this morning. When they finished the puzzle, they left it on the table. Mary said she was tired and needed to rest. He kissed her on the cheek. She retired to his room, taking Tad, under considerable protest, to his. As always, Tad wanted to stay up with his father, but Mr. Lincoln said it was bedtime for everybody, including himself.

He went to his room to sleep alone. He and Mary no longer slept in the passionate bed of their youths. They slept the restless sleep of late middle age now, with its tossing and turning, snoring, and frequent trips to the chamber pot. In all too short a time, he expected it to become the restless sleep of old age.

I must complete my life's work of saving the Union and ending slavery now, so that when the time comes, I will join the sleep of my fathers in peace. I will find no peace if I allow these controversies to roil future generations. Tad's generation must not die in agonies in muddy trenches and foul prison camps, as our generation is dying. My generation has made this war and we must end it, by prevailing over slavery and disunion, now, and for all time to come.

When he got to his room, he closed the door, undressed, and put on his cotton nightclothes. He raised the windows quarter-way to let in the draft. It had gotten cooler and less humid after the passing of the storm.

Two more weeks, and the first touch of the beautiful dry days of autumn will commence. Perhaps by then things will look better.

He reflected on the events of the day as he sat on the edge of the bed peering out at lamplit Washington. The smell of smoke wafted in, with the scent of roasting pork and brewing coffee. It came from the men of the Ohio regiment camping on the lawn. He could hear them talking.

Though he could not make out their words, he could tell by their laughter that it was the happy talk of men who had done their duty during a crisis and were on their way back to the comfort and familiarity of their homes.

He felt this was a momentous day, but its full impact was just beyond his grasp. He lay down and closed his eyes, falling into the pleasant reverie that precedes unconsciousness. During those moments he recalled his life in the complete way of one much nearer its end than its beginning.

He relived one of his first happy memories of the Kentucky hills where he'd been born --- of running into the cool spring in the cave during summer days of soaking humidity; of days spent with his beloved mother and sister, who passed away before he left home. He remembered the excitement of learning to read as taught by an itinerant teacher in a backwoods schoolhouse; of discovering the big world beyond the little frontier clearing, in places and times going back to the beginning of Man. He remembered his inspirations from Mason Weems' *Life of George Washington*, and the Bible, whose wisdom was eternal.

He remembered his youthful years of adventure, of flat-boating down the Mississippi to New Orleans and enlisting in the militia to fight Blackhawk's War. There was his rise to prominence in Springfield; then engaging with Stephen Douglas in the remarkable coincidence of the nation's two most influential men residing in the same frontier town. He remembered being defeated by Douglas in the Senate election of 1858, then prevailing over Douglas' shattered party in 1860. He and Douglas married Southern women from slave-holding families. Douglas had sided with the slave owners for far too long, then made amends after the war started by rendering his full assistance to Lincoln. He passed away two months later knowing the government was being administered faithfully to preserve the Union.

Stephen Douglas is gone now, and the old world he represented is fading. The world will be reborn between now and the next century. It will be reborn either as a free world that harnesses machinery for the betterment of Man, or for his enslavement. We must not come down on the side of enslavement!

He awoke from his musings long enough to observe his magnificent room, visible dimly in the glow of the soldiers' campfires outside. He smiled as he thought about how far up in life he'd come. Not so long ago, he'd ridden horseback through dusty Illinois prairie towns, following the itinerant circuit courts by day, and sharing flea-infested beds with other itinerant lawyers in packed rooms by night. Now his days and nights were graced with conversations of momentous import among the most renowned people in the land. Even so, they did not quite come up to those boisterous good times he'd had arguing legal cases and politics around the fireplaces in those crowded little taverns.

He fell asleep dreaming about those happy fire-lit conversations on a late winter's night in the 1850s. Perhaps the voices that filtered through his sleep were those of the soldiers billeted outside his window, celebrating their return to their homes.

The Days After

Lincoln's decisions on August 23rd ,1864 inclined the Union towards victory. Foremost among their effects was the renewal of confidence in himself. The Republican National Committee, chaired by Henry Raymond in New York, was having second thoughts about nominating him for a second term. His reversal of his decision to designate Raymond as a peace commissioner was delivered by John Nicolay on August 25th. It had the desired effect of stiffening the Committee's spines and inducing them to repose their trust in his ability to conclude the war on terms of Union victory.

Nicolay wrote to John Hay:

"I think that today is the turning point in our crisis. If the President can infect Raymond and his committee with some of his own patience and pluck, we are saved. If our friends will only rub their eyes and shake themselves and become convinced that they themselves are not dead, we shall win the fight overwhelmingly."

The historian of the Republican National Committee declared:

"Encouraged and cheered, the committee issued an optimistic statement of confidence in Lincoln's reelection...and the [New York] Times next day denied that the Government had any thought of peace negotiations. Its sole and undivided purpose is to prosecute the war until the rebellion is quelled."

The abandonment of the delusion of negotiated peace stiffened the Union armies in Virginia and Georgia. Men died and were crippled by combat and disease as much as before, but desertions lessened and surrenders became less perfunctory. Men enlisted and re-enlisted a little more readily, while the quality and resolve of enlistees improved. The Army of the Potomac still lost two men for every one removed from General Lee's army, but the rate of replacement began to exceed the loss. Lee's army declined relative to Grant's.

Declining the prisoner exchanges was one of Mr. Lincoln's toughest decisions, because it went against his sense of humanity. He knew it would cost the lives of thousands of his men, who had heeded his call to fight for the Union. Yet, he judged that for every life that might be saved by a prisoner exchange, another life, and more, would be lost fighting the prolonged Rebellion.

Had the prisoner exchange resumed in August 1864, both sides would have received tens of thousands of enfeebled men. The war would have stopped for weeks while Union ships transported their debilitated men out of the South and quartermasters strained to supply rations to restore their health, while also keeping the active-duty armies fed and equipped. Many released Union prisoners would have been discharged due to illness or expired enlistment terms. The Confederates would also have received their men back in poor health. But fighting on the defensive in fortified positions, for the cause of national independence, and being enlisted for the duration of the war, their return to service would have provided a significant relative advantage.

Resuming the prisoner exchange would have advanced the idea that peace was imminent. This may have implied a lack of confidence in Mr. Lincoln's ability to see the war through to a successful conclusion and inclined more people to vote for McClellan. Desertions would have increased and cajoling unwilling conscripts and bounty jumpers into the army would have become more difficult.

Declining Illinois Governor Yates' request for four regiments of veterans to occupy Springfield also proved wise. The Copperhead Conspiracy in Illinois was larger than Lincoln knew; but, like its namesake reptile, was not large enough to become dangerous unless provoked. The Copperheads might have caused substantial trouble if he sent Federal troops to Springfield to assist Yates in harassing Democratic voters and politicians. Absent provocations of those sorts, the Copperheads shouted unsavory epithets against Lincoln, but did not field armed paramilitary forces Confederate agents hoped to forge into a new Confederate army operating in Illinois and Indiana.

Perhaps even more damaging would have been the ridicule: "What's the matter, Abe? You have to bring in the army to keep the Rebels out of your own home?" That alone might have cost him the election.

He did unobtrusively direct Stanton to route the returned Hundred Days Men through trouble spots. This put Yates, Morton, and other excitable "War Governors" at ease during that tense autumn of 1864. And he endorsed the unauthorized transfer of funds from Stanton's War Department to Yates' and Morton's personal accounts to keep their governments operating without the consent of their Copperhead legislatures.

He decided not to annoy Sherman with a request for a report on his situation down in Georgia. If the high-strung Sherman had any failing, it was being touchy about being second-guessed. Atlanta fell to Sherman's army on September 2nd. He did not interfere with Sherman's plan to abandon his supply line after capturing Atlanta, then marching through the heart of Georgia. The Confederates were still fighting hard. Had they stalled Sherman's men in Middle Georgia, Sherman's army, lacking re-supply, might have been in danger. Though anxious, he did not prohibit Sherman's March to the Sea that proved the Confederacy could no longer defend its heartland.

His other incidental business on the 23rd was thanking the Ohio Regiment of Hundred Days Men, but not hectoring them to extend their enlistment. They went home in a happy spirit and voted almost unanimously to re-elect him.

His routine patience in answering the concerns of people with such diverse views as Charles D. Robinson, Henry Raymond, and Frederick Douglass, kept the pro-Union factions behind him sufficiently united to see the war through to victory. Had he lost patience with any of these factions and responded in the same impatient and dictatorial tone they often beseeched him, he would have lost their trust.

At home he'd had patience to love his temperamental wife and help her contribute to the war effort. She was adored by radical abolitionist firebrand Senator Charles Sumner, thereby lessening the Radicals' animosity to Mr. Lincoln, who they castigated as being too slow to emancipate the slaves, and too lenient on the Rebels. Her work on behalf of wounded soldiers and indigent former slaves endeared her to the ordinary people of Washington, even if she was despised in social circles. Her devotion to the Union and to the liberation of Negroes who'd once been her family's slaves, won her husband many votes.

His most important act of mercy that day was the sparing of Mr. Bohm. Had he allowed the execution to stand, the news would have spread. People would have said, "The cruel tyrant is killing old men now." Because of these routine acts of mercy, fair-minded people in the North became prone to saying: "Lincoln has responded with the necessary authority required to restore the Union. In doing so, he and his administrators were bound to make some unwise decisions. Perhaps his men, on occasion, have been too quick to arrest people on the thinnest suspicions of disloyalty. Mistakes of this kind are to be expected in the haste and waste of war. But Mr. Lincoln is not a tyrant."

These factors together swung the election of November 8, 1864 his way. He won 55% of the North's popular vote and 212 electoral votes vs. McClellan's 45% of the popular vote and 23 electoral votes. He lost only Kentucky, New Jersey, and Delaware. But even with events breaking in his favor, it was close in several important states. He won New York State by only one half of one percent; Pennsylvania and Connecticut by a percent and a half; Indiana, Illinois, and New Hampshire with around 54% of the vote. Had he made poor decisions on the 23rd the election would have been far less favorable. A narrower win would have discouraged the North and encouraged the Confederates, while an outright loss would have brought in George McClellan, who'd been Jefferson Davis' protégé before the war.

If Mr. Lincoln had lost the election, he would have had to carry on for four months (until the 20th Amendment was ratified in 1933 new presidents were not inaugurated until the following March) as a discredited president.

His best hope might have been to offer McClellan his job back as Commander-in-Chief of the Union Armies. That would have united the two great leaders of the North in a common effort to defeat the Rebellion. However, Grant would have been demoted. Furthermore, McClellan disrespected Lincoln. The Radical Republicans, who thought Mr. Lincoln far too easy on the Rebels, despised McClellan, whose attitude toward the Rebels was much more benign than Lincoln's. It would have been difficult for an incoming President McClellan and an outgoing President Lincoln to work together to win the war. The Northern public might have seen the defeat of Mr. Lincoln as proof of a failed war, and the Northern armies might have dissolved.

It is possible that even the one half of one percent victory in New York by itself may have made the difference between defeat and victory in the war. If New York, by far the largest state in population and economic power, had voted against Lincoln, then perhaps its governor and legislature, and those of other wavering states, would have suspended their support of the war.

Mr. Lincoln's wise decisions convinced the Northern people that casting him aside in favor of McClellan was not worth the risk of turning a winning war into a losing one.

About the Story

This story began when I wrote two articles for **Civil War Times Illustrated Magazine** for its December 1981 special edition *Dissent: Fire in the Rear*. One of my articles told the story of how Copperheads were elected to majorities in the Illinois and Indiana legislatures, and how Governors Yates and Morton employed extra-constitutional means to constrain them. I discovered aspects of the Civil War I had never seen popularized, especially that the Union cause hung by such a thin thread until August 1864.

As to the particulars of this story, it is a novelized version of historically documented events. The letters and Mr. Lincoln's memorandums to himself are all shown as they were written. Most of Mr. Lincoln's conversations are either documented as having been said or have been taken from his letters and speeches.

The story of the paroled Union sergeants from Andersonville who Mr. Lincoln declined to see is mentioned in several sources:

http://law2.umkc.edu/Faculty/projects/ftrials/Wirz/anders1.htm

The conditions [at Andersonville] were so poor that in July 1864 Captain Wirz [Confederate Commandant] paroled five Union soldiers to deliver a petition signed by the majority of Andersonville's prisoners asking that the Union reinstate prisoner exchanges. The request in the petition was denied and the Union soldiers, who had sworn to do so, returned to report this to their comrades.

John Ransom, Quartermaster of Company A, 9th Michigan Volunteer Cavalry, captured in November 1863, tells the story of the "men paroled on honor" to urgently plead for the resumption of the exchange, in his book *John Ransom's Andersonville Diary:*

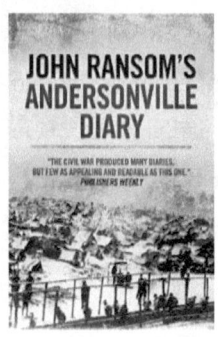

July 22. — A petition is gotten up, signed by all the Sergeants in the prison, to be sent to Washington, D. C., begging to be released. Captain Wirtz has consented to let three representatives go for that purpose. Rough that it should be necessary for us to beg to be protected by our Government.

July 23. — Reports of an exchange in August. Can't stand it till that time. Will soon go up the spout.

He tells of the mounting death toll:

July 27. — Sweltering hot. No worse than yesterday. Said that two hundred die now each day. Howe very bad and Sanders getting so. Swan dead, Gordon dead, Jack Withers dead, Scotty dead, a large Irishman who has been near us a long time, is dead. These and scores of others died yesterday and day before. Hub Dakin came to see me and brought an onion. He is just able to crawl around himself.

Aug. 2 — Two hundred and twenty die each day. No more news of exchange.

The rumors of pending exchanges kept the prisoners alive with hope:

Aug. 29. — Exchange rumors afloat. Any kind of a change would help me.

Ransom, John L. John Ransom's Andersonville Diary (pp. 68-71). Roland Books. Kindle Edition.

Ransom was one of the fortunate survivors. The Confederates moved him to a hospital in Savannah, as they began to move prisoners out of the makeshift Andersonville camp and into permanent camps that were less crowded and more sanitary. Transfer to these less deadly prison camps came too late for the 12,930 Union men who perished at Andersonville, about four times as many as died fighting for the Union at Gettysburg. Ransom understood, and disagreed with, Grant's and Lincoln's decision not to exchange them:

Oct. 9. — The reason we have not been exchanged is because if the exchange is made, it will put all the men held by the Union forces right into the Rebel army, while the Union prisoners of war held by the Rebels are in no condition to do service; that would seem to me to be a very poor reason [for not exchanging us].

Ransom, John L. John Ransom's Andersonville Diary (p. 79). Roland Books. Kindle Edition.

General Grant explained his reasons for not resuming the prisoner exchanges: https://ehistory.osu.edu/books/official-records/120/0607

"It is hard on our men held in Southern prisons not to exchange them, but it is humanity to those left in the ranks to fight our battles.

Every man we hold, when released on parole or otherwise, becomes an active soldier against us at once either directly or indirectly. If we commence a system of exchange which liberates all prisoners taken, we will have to fight on until the whole South is exterminated. If we hold those caught, they amount to no more than dead men. At this particular time to release all rebel prisoners North would ensure Sherman's defeat and would compromise our safety here." – General Ulysses S. Grant, August 18, 1864.

Ransom explains that the Lincoln Administration's refusal to resume the prisoner exchanges in 1864 convinced him to "vote" for George McClellan during the prisoners' mock election:

Nov. 6. — One year ago to-day captured. Presidential election at the North between Lincoln and McClellan…. I voted for McClellan with a hurrah, and another hurrah, and still another. Had this election occurred while we were at Andersonville, four-fifth would have voted for McClellan. We think ourselves shamefully treated, in being left so long as prisoners of war. Abe Lincoln is a good man, and a good President, but he is controlled by others who rule the exchange business, as well as most other things. Had lots of fun hurrahing for "Little Mac." [George McClellan]

Ransom, John L.. John Ransom's Andersonville Diary (p. 87). Roland Books. Kindle Edition.

Another aspect of Andersonville is the staggering number of Federal soldiers being captured in 1864. The beginning of this story tells of news reaching Lincoln on August 23 of the Battle of the Weldon Railroad (also known as Globe Tavern) where nearly 3,000 Union men surrendered while capturing only about 400 Confederates. If the

Federals had continued surrendering in those numbers, they would have lost the war as their armies melted away faster than they could be replenished. Mr. Lincoln's decision not to talk peace with the Confederates, or to resume the prisoner exchanges, may have reduced the surrenders sufficiently to provide the margin Grant needed to prevail in his war of attrition.

The story of Mr. Bohm being sentenced to execution for desertion is a composite of several cases. Mr. Lincoln really did inquire about one deserter's marital status. When informed that the man was married, he said: "Send him back to his wife. In a year he'll wish I'd let him be shot.".

The story of governors Richard Yates and Oliver P. Morton suspending their pro-Confederate legislatures in Illinois and Indiana happened as described. Richard Yates employed a dubious technicality to "prorogue" (disband) the Illinois Legislature for two years, while Oliver P. Morton asked the Republican legislatures to boycott Indiana's legislature, thereby depriving it of a quorum to conduct business. Lacking the legally required appropriations by their legislatures, Yates and Morton operated their states on an informal basis by voluntary contributions and loans from Edwin Stanton's War Department. Stanton was warned that the War Department money was not the legal way to fund state governments, and that all involved would be "covered with prosecutions if the Cause fails." Stanton replied: "If the cause fails, I do not wish to live."

I discovered after writing this book that Lincoln did discuss with Stanton and Grant the possibility of using conscription to create another army in 1864 to be landed on North Carolina's coast and then come up through inland North Carolina to threaten Lee's army in Virginia from its undefended southern approaches. The difficulty by then was that there were not enough competent officers left to command a new army. Sending the conscripts to continue Grant's bloody war of attrition in Virginia, though it increased the Northern people's war weariness, was judged the more prudent option to conclude the war.

General Lew Wallace's poignant story is true. He never overcame his mortification at being blamed for the near-debacle of Shiloh. He was driven to write *Ben Hur,* based on his own story of blame and redemption. It became the most popular novel of the late Nineteenth Century.

The story of Lincoln's delicate handling of Sherman is true. Sherman was relieved of command early in the war for making the "hysterical" comment that it would require 200,000 men to put down the Rebellion in the Mississippi Valley alone. Later, it became clear that Sherman had, if anything, underestimated the manpower required. At the end of the war, he was nearly relieved of command again, by order of President Andrew Johnson and Secretary of State Stanton, for agreeing to an armistice, instead of a formal surrender, with his pre-war friend Confederate General Joseph Johnston. Sherman was a volatile personality. Had Mr. Lincoln tried to micromanage him in 1864, he may have severely undermined the Union's cause.

Decades later, Sherman passed away and was buried on a blustery winter day. Joseph Johnston was one of the pall bearers. "Put on your hat, or you'll catch your death of cold!" advised Sherman's widow. Joe Johnston refused to disrespect his deceased friend by putting on his hat. "Sherman would not put on his hat if he was carrying my remains," he replied. Old Joe Johnston did indeed catch pneumonia and died shortly after burying his friend in peace, and respected enemy in war. The tragedy of the Civil War is that it set such men against each other.

Finally, there is Frederick Douglass. His intelligence, wisdom, and measured appeals for justice for Negroes gave living proof to refute the Southern belief that Negroes were fit only to work as field hands and servants. His message, in essence, was:

"Negroes do not ask for any special favors. Just set us free, and we will take care of ourselves, like all other free people."

He inspired many Union-men to understand the dual purposes of the war, which were to restore the Union and liberate African Americans. Slaves were not to be freed only to become oppressed in lesser ways, but to become American citizens with full civil rights. That promise would be delayed another century, but there would be no more talk of expelling American Africans from the country.

About the Author

"Understanding history is a key to understanding the present and extrapolating the future."

- Alan Sewell

I've devoted my life to analyzing historical and current events and applying their historical lessons to today's business and economic issues.

Although every day is a new day, the new days are layered on top of repeating cycles of history as old as Mankind. The more we understand the cycles of history, the more complete our understanding of the present will be.

My writing is focused on American History. It starts with my lifelong fascination with the Civil War, the crucible that defined us as a nation. This was a lively topic of discussion in our house growing up, as my mother was raised in Middle Georgia in the 1930s, hearing stories her grandparents experienced as children during Sherman's March, and watching parades by the last of the ancient Confederate veterans; her four great grandfathers having fought for the Confederacy, whose traditions were alive to her and passed down to me.

My father's Civil War ancestors were North Alabama Appalachian hill country Unionists, some having enlisted in the 1st Alabama Cavalry, **USA** that fought for the Union and committed depredations against Confederates in Georgia during Sherman's March, in retaliation for the Confederates' oppression of Alabama Unionists. He was raised in the tradition of White Southern Unionists who were proud of Southern traditions but did not think well of the Confederacy.

I thus learned about both sides of the Civil War early in life and continued studying it, especially its politics and political dissent. Having lived in Alabama, Georgia, Florida, Ohio, Kentucky, Illinois, New York, and Michigan, I understand how the conflict is seen from both sides of the Ohio River. I began writing about it in university with two articles that created the December 1981 *Civil War Times Illustrated* Special issue: DISSENT: FIRE IN THE REAR. These articles chronicled the dissent of the Unionist minority in North Alabama against the Confederacy, and the dissent by Illinois Copperheads against President Lincoln's government. I then wrote other novels and nonfiction about the Civil War with a view toward exploring intriguing aspects of civil and military events that have not been well-told.

Other Books by Alan Sewell

Fire in the Heartland is a novelized true story of the entire Civil War, as seen from the perspective of Mary Lincoln's cousins, who bought through the war on opposite sides in Kentucky, Alabama, and Illinois:

https://www.amazon.com/ebook/dp/B0051 4WNYG/

Fire in the Heartland: A Civil War Novel of the Decision that Won the Civil War Hardcover – December 17, 2021
by Alan Sewell (Author)
4.0 ★★★★☆ (28)   See all formats and editions

FIRE IN THE HEARTLAND is a novelized true story that fills in the gaps of our knowledge about little-known events that decided the outcome of the Civil War. The story was obscured after the war and largely forgotten. Its retelling is based on research originally published in popular history magazines that brings the events to life. It provides a unique insight into the personal and political intrigues that were part of the war. And it's a great read.

- Fire in the Heartland gives us a different perspective on the Civil War. As a career military officer, I saw Generals McClellan, Grant, Sherman, Jackson, Lee and others portrayed in different lights. I felt the horrible decisions made by both sides as they tried to protect their territories, find manpower for their armies and limit travel in the young nation as it slowly divided itself. I saw how close Lincoln came to loosing reelection and how close McClellan came to winning the Presidency. Had that happened, our nation today would look very different.

- Fire in the Heartland takes the reader into the levels of the War that are seldom seen. Family divisions have been portrayed before, but the depth of the political intrigue has always needed to be exposed and is done quite interestingly.
⌄ Read more

-Fire in the Heartland gives us a different perspective on the Civil War. As a career military officer, I saw Generals McClellan, Grant, Sherman, Jackson, Lee, and others portrayed in different lights. I felt the horrible decisions made by both sides as they tried to protect their territories, find manpower for their armies and limit travel in the young nation as it slowly divided itself. I saw how close Lincoln came to loosing reelection and how close McClellan came to winning the Presidency. Had that happened, our nation today would look very different.

- Fire in the Heartland takes the reader into the levels of the War that are seldom seen. The development of the opposing factions, in my opinion, exceeded that of the mini-series 'The Blue and The Gray'. Family divisions have been portrayed before, but the depth of the political intrigue

has always needed to be exposed and is done quite interestingly and provocatively.... overall a very enjoyable and educational read."

- A vivid account of the political turmoil within ordinary families and the nation at large before, during, and after the Civil War!-An interesting historical novel and an easy read. The Civil War and the way it fractured families was a very difficult time in our history. I thought this was well presented by the author.

- I must say that I both enjoyed the book, and learned much by reading it, and I, a former history teacher, recommend it highly.

- I enjoyed the entire premise of the book. It gives you a different, but very informative, look at the entire war. I enjoyed it very much!

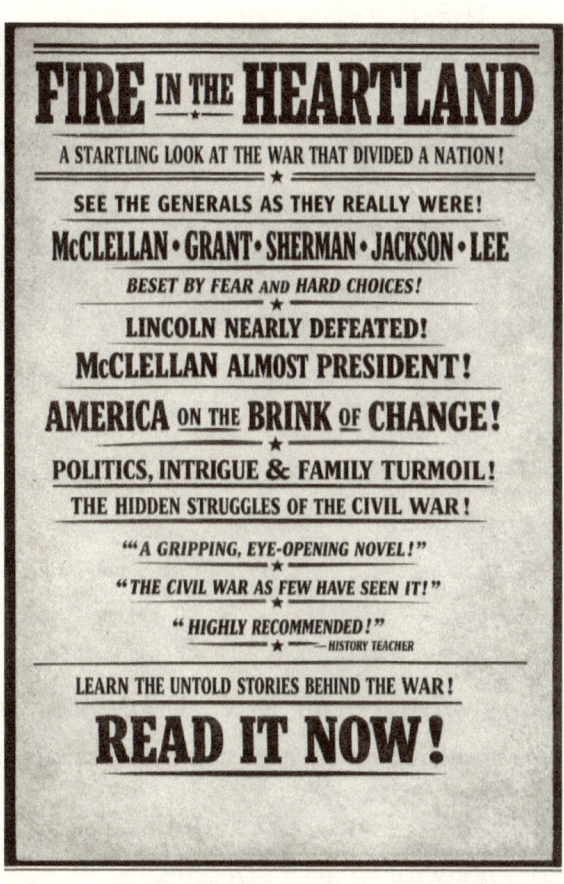

FIRE IN THE HEARTLAND

A STARTLING LOOK AT THE WAR THAT DIVIDED A NATION!

★

SEE THE GENERALS AS THEY REALLY WERE!

McCLELLAN • GRANT • SHERMAN • JACKSON • LEE

BESET BY FEAR AND HARD CHOICES!

★

LINCOLN NEARLY DEFEATED!

McCLELLAN ALMOST PRESIDENT!

AMERICA ON THE BRINK OF CHANGE!

★

POLITICS, INTRIGUE & FAMILY TURMOIL!

THE HIDDEN STRUGGLES OF THE CIVIL WAR!

"A GRIPPING, EYE-OPENING NOVEL!"

★

"THE CIVIL WAR AS FEW HAVE SEEN IT!"

★

" HIGHLY RECOMMENDED!"

★ ——— HISTORY TEACHER

LEARN THE UNTOLD STORIES BEHIND THE WAR!

READ IT NOW!

If you like alternate history speculations that help us understand real history, you might enjoy reading my *Confederate Union*. It presumes that the Democrats united their party around a slavery-expansionist platform in 1860 that won the election. In that althist scenario, Mr. Lincoln must decide whether he should maintain his loyalty to the Union or lead The Rebellion of the Free State North.

www.amazon.com/dp/B00AKG0LZI/

www.amazon.com/gp/product/B00GLHV8IY/

www.amazon.com/dp/B00RC08EBS/

www.amazon.com/dp/B07J3NGCFD/

The Diary of American Exceptionalism is an analysis of American History focusing on six critical turning points, including the Civil War.

https://www.amazon.com/ebook/dp/B01H2HGCNC/

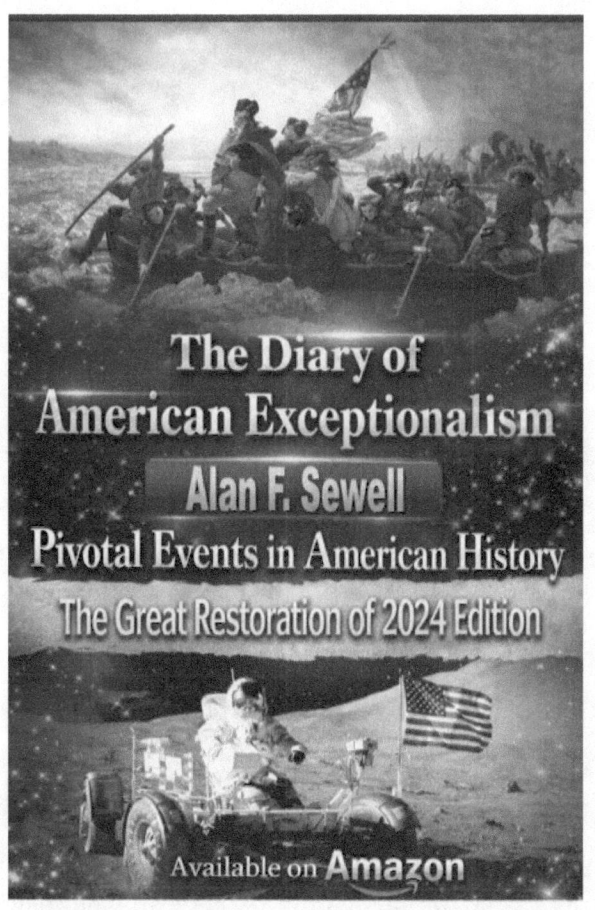

"If we could first know where we are, and whither we are tending, we could better judge what to do, and how to do it."

So said Abraham Lincoln as he contemplated the great issues of containing slavery and preserving the Union. This book is written to show where we are, and whither we may be tending, by explaining our current political controversies in context of where we have been at similar crisis points in the past.

It is written as a distilled essence of American history, explained in the words of the people who made it. It focuses narrowly but intensively on six periods of quantum change that moved us into new political and economic directions. Since it appears that we may be at another turning point in our history, it may provide insights into our future direction.

This book focuses on the five previous critical periods of our history that reshaped the country and relates them to the sixth that we are now experiencing:

Fragmentation — Federalism — Union (1783-1815) was our first existential crisis testing whether we would squander our Independence by fragmenting into warring factions, thereby allowing most of our territory to be reabsorbed back into the British, French, and

Spanish empires. Ultimately, our Founders' vision of a continent-spanning Republic, governed by democratic principles, prevailed.

Secession — War — Nationalism (1858-1867) tested whether we were a Union of sovereign states that were free to resume their independence at will, or a union of individuals under a sovereign national government superior to the states.

Wealth — Depression — Empire (1890-1900) After the Civil War, the United States developed our industrial economy while advancing the frontier to the Pacific Coast. However, the development was not sustainable. We suffered our first great depression in 1894-1897. Unemployment, hunger, and rioting disrupted our cities and required suppression by the army. We became aware that a modern urban / industrial economy develops instabilities that require moderation by government. However, the reform agendas of that era were short-circuited by the fever for overseas expansion, that took us far beyond our North American homeland and made us a global power.

Wealth — Depression — Liberalism (1929-1934). Our economy revived and generally prospered between 1900 and 1929. It took on its modern look and feel with production of automobiles, appliances, national radio broadcasts, the mass migration of farm workers to cities, and the migration of city people to suburbs. Then it all came crashing down in 1929 due to an imbalance between production and consumption. Franklin Roosevelt's New Deal rebalanced the economy by bolstering consumption and tamping back excess investment in production and unsound speculation in financial assets.

Chaos — Humiliation — Conservatism (1968-1980). The 1960's were destined to be chaotic. Social unrest at home, a deteriorating economy, and our failure to defeat the communists in South Vietnam, led many to believe the United States was in decline. The election of Ronald Reagan, who campaigned on free market principles, revived our economy, and remade much of the world in our image. We also put our values fully into practice at home by ending racial segregation and discrimination and granting full civil rights to our African American citizens.

Globalism — Great Recession — {Populism or Progressivism?}: (2008-2020) Some "Cycles of History" historians believe we are entering a sixth pivot point, as demonstrated by the rise of unconventional new candidates on the Populist Right and Progressive Left. We may be able to forecast our future direction by comparing this period to previous pivot points in our history.

Feedback

Please address feedback to alsnewideas@gmail.com